MURDER IN ROSSLARE

MURDER
IN ROSSLARE

Kin Platt

Walker and Company
New York

For Joan Garnett

First published in the United States of America in 1986 by the Walker Publishing Company, Inc.

Published simultaneously in Canada by John Wiley & Sons Canada, Limited, Rexdale, Ontario.

ISBN 0-8027-5639-5

Printed in the United States of America

10 9 8 7 6 5 4 3 2 1

PART ONE
One

Dublin was behind him now, but not the rain. Stanwood shifted his formidable bulk, uncomfortable with the narrow-seated confines of the small black and tan CIE train rattling south. A fixed table was set between the facing seats throughout the car, a convenience for playing cards, propping a newspaper or package, or taking lunch; but Stanwood had none of these, and as the train jolted and jerked, he swore silently, glowering as he tried to distribute his oversize body by leaning to the side, easing his cramped and aching midriff off the sharp edge of the cursed table.

Blasted train is for midgets, he thought sourly. The other passengers he viewed on the opposite aisle seemed complacent, showing no visible annoyance. Well, and why not, he thought. They're used to these damn toy cars. Probably been bred to fit.

The steady rain that had left him sodden in Dublin increased in intensity, and the spattered windows offered only a blurred panorama of the bleak countryside. The train ran parallel and close to the Irish Sea from Dun Laoghaire to Wicklow, and he saw it vast and murky into the distance, the long curling waves approaching to break gently on the dark wet strand.

Gusts of wind swept through the open windows, jammed stuck, of the swaying car, and the chill of the October morning seeped into Stanwood's bones. The other occupants, he noticed, wore heavy coats, collars turned up, hats and down-padded anoraks. Some were already breaking out the thermos jugs of hot tea, as Stanwood watched enviously. So much for the sunny southeast, he thought, rubbing at his heavy thighs, slapping his numbed knees together. Let's hope it's better at Rosslare.

He was a stranger to Ireland, knew next to nothing of the country, but he was more than a casual tourist. The long flight from Los Angeles to New York, followed by the even longer Aer Lingus night flight to Dublin airport through Shannon was no tentative vacation. Nor was it a business trip, as Stanwood was no longer in business. For more than half his life he had been a detective of homicide with the Los Angeles Police Department, and now he had given it up for retirement. After Kate's death, his work had no more meaning for him than living itself, and the trip now was for Kate, to honour a commitment.

There was the younger sister, Noreen, who had remained when Kate had left Ireland forever for the States over twenty years ago. The parents had exerted some hold on the child, and she had never followed Kate over. Promises to visit had been made, and never kept. The years rolled by and all that Stanwood knew of Noreen Kelly had been gleaned from the meagre correspondence between the sisters, an occasional photograph taken during early school years. A rare postcard, brief note, then nothing.

Kate Kelly had come on straight to California, found herself a job and a husky young giant pounding the Los Angeles streets as a policeman, married him, encouraged him into bettering his grade and becoming a detective; loved him with a fanaticism that defied all reason, and died suddenly, never older than the day they met, Stanwood believed, and left him desolate, a grieving lost hulk of a man.

Her one continuing concern had been for her younger sister, to see her well, and before she died the pact had been mutely made that Stanwood would look in on her, help the girl if he could. His fingers rubbed at the worn ring in his pocket. That, along with many pictures of Kate and their years together, and the stories he could tell of her warmth, dedication and final moments, was what he was bringing to Noreen Kelly in Rosslare. All that a man could do.

Stanwood blinked, unaware that his eyes had moistened. It took the merest fragment of memory to break him down again, and he shook his head, rubbed his face with the large battered knuckles that betrayed the inherent violence of his profession, marvelling as always at the tenacity of his one all-consuming love.

To break the sentimental chain of his thoughts, he faced the rain-streaked window to look inland at the lush rolling hills of County Wicklow. The emerald-green fields glistened damply, dotted with an occasional stone house, smoke curling from turf fires through squat red chimneys. Horses stood with bowed heads, flanks to the slanting rain; cattle huddled in the middle of yellow-green meadows. Washing hung stiffly behind the houses. There were thatched roofs on small white cottages, ploughs and tractors alongside barns.

It was early enough for people to be stirring. A lighted room suggested a man and wife having breakfast. Children were running out of doors and he looked searchingly ahead for schools, perhaps buses. A child of his own, he thought, would have been no use to him now, reminding him always of the mother. And yet, how wonderful and fruitful it might have been. To watch the seedling sprout, the growing miracle every day.

And then it's out of the nest for good, he reminded himself harshly, and you'd be on your own again, a fool of a man with no understanding of the ways of nature.

People were something else. His years as a police officer had acquainted him with all kinds, the good and passive along with the crazies and violent ones. It had taken long hard years to absorb the feel for them, the patience to withhold judgment until the pertinent facts had been assembled and weighed. He thought he knew people now. Only to himself did Stanwood remain an imponderable mystery.

From Wicklow to Arklow, the train fled from the grey-green Irish Sea. There were ruins in the hills, stumps of Norman castles. Beyond Rathdrum, he strained to see the Vale of Avoca, checking hastily with his map, but in the downpour it could have been anything. The sea came into view again after Arklow, and then he was being carried inland, seeing little villages, a pub, a church, petrol stations and clusters of streets.

People were getting about in small cars, lorries were filling the narrow roads. There were more little houses set far apart, a man kissing his woman goodbye at an open door. She wore a brown scarf over red hair. Stanwood swallowed hard.

The wizened old conductor was shaking his shoulder, yelling something down at him. Stanwood looked up stupidly. "What?" he said. "What's that?"

The old man was jabbing at the air toward the front of the car. "It's Rosslare coming up, sir. You'll be the one asking for it."

Stanwood shook himself. "Amen," he said.

Two

The train pulled away leaving him on the open, desolate platform. Rain lashed at him as Stanwood looked around trying to get his bearings. The hotel in Dublin had called ahead to arrange the Rosslare reservation, but there was nobody to meet him. Up ahead was a small bridge and road passing across the tracks. Stanwood shook water off his head, wondering which direction to try.

A trainman was leaving a shed at the far end. Stanwood watched him approach a small parked car. He waved his arm at the man.

"Can you direct me to the Strand Hotel?"

The trainman was young, smiling. "I'll do better. It's on me way, not far. Hop in. I'll take you there."

Stanwood forced his bulk and bag into the tiny car, grateful for the lift. "Damn nice of you. I've no idea where they're hiding the blasted place."

The driver backed and turned up a narrow lane Stanwood hadn't noticed. "Just over the ridge here. The strand is the beach along the water, you know."

The little car hummed over the hill and turned down a narrow blacktop road. "Why is everything so small here?" Stanwood said, trying to keep the weight of his shoulders off the man.

The driver laughed. His blue trainman suit was worn and shiny. "Well, you'll be too big for most of it, that's a fact. Although we have some large men, too, you'll be seeing. As for the cars, it's a small country, and we've no need for bigger ones. Saves on the petrol, too, you know, and what with the cost of it, we do far better this way." He patted the steering wheel with affection. "You'll be coming from the States, man?"

"Los Angeles."

"Aye, I've heard of the place." He cut in sharply and the car skidded through water. "Now," he said.

Stanwood looked at him. "What?"

The man pointed over Stanwood's shoulder. "There's your hotel. Good luck with you."

"Much obliged," Stanwood said, hauling himself out. He stood for a moment waving his thanks at the departing car and driver, unmoved by the pelting rain. Then he found the entrance and stepped inside the glass door.

Immediately on his left was a large parlour with a fireplace blazing. People were reclining on soft chairs. The warmth of the fire flooded across the open door and he was tempted to duck in, dry himself, get the chill out of his bones. But the check-in counter was just ahead down the hall. He might as well get that over with first, he decided. See that his reservation was in order.

He squished soddenly past men and women looking comfortably dry, warmed by sweater or coat. A blonde girl at the reception desk looked up at him. Stanwood removed his hat and water dripped on the counter. The girl was decent about it, acting as if she had seen rainwater before.

"Sorry about that. My name is Stanwood. The manager of the Berkeley Court in Dublin made a reservation for me here."

She glanced down at her reservation book. "Oh, Mr. Stanwood, I'm so sorry. We were to meet you at the station but your train is in early." She turned to a big clock on the wall. "You're not due in Rosslare until 11:15 – and look at you, man – you're soaking wet."

I've been wet before, he thought. The question is, do you have the room for me? "No problem. I can get into dry things if you have the room ready."

She handed him a key. Attached to it was a huge plastic disc. It'd be hard to lose that one, he thought. "Room 26," she said crisply. "It's all prepared. Second floor, top of the stairs. And you can use the warming room just below."

His shoulders swung back, shedding more water. "Warming room?"

"To dry your wet clothes. The girl will show you."

He was at the stairs with his bag, when the girl called. "Mind your head, sir, at the first turn, top of the stairs."

Stanwood shrugged, walking up the short flight. He was looking at the key in his hand. He recoiled, stopped short, grunting at the word generally used when bonking one's head.

"Are you all right?" the girl asked.

"What?" he said. "It's okay. Just a little bump." He rubbed his forehead, and with bent knees and hunched shoulders looked at the offending slanted stairwell overhead. Now if I do that every day, he thought, I'll be a lot shorter when I leave; That could take your head off.

He stepped cautiously into his room. There was sufficient head clearance. No beams overhead to bonk against. It was a brightly coloured room, lit with a soft glow from the sea. Small bath and shower. The bed was firm, comfortable enough for his size. He went to the window, looked out across low tarred rooftops, auxiliary wings of the hotel. There was a thin strand of deserted beach beyond. Nothing to be seen on the dull green sea. The rain had eased to a soft persistent drizzle.

He stripped and took a hot shower. Towelled dry, he unpacked his bag and put on dry clothes. He took his wet outer clothing out to the hall. A thin girl wearing a green dress was polishing the head of the staircase.

"Warming room?" he asked, awkwardly showing his wet things.

"Just below, sir. Next half-landing. Right through the door."

"I mean, what is it? What do you do with the stuff?"

Her voice was light, with a lilt of the brogue. "Why, you hang them up to dry, sir. The room is heated, you see."

It was a musty-smelling room, small and uncomfortably hot. Coats, hats, pants and mackintoshes hung over thick steaming pipes. Stanwood moved a few items, and found room for his own. As he balanced his hat on the top, he wondered briefly if the heat would shrink its brim. Well, the hell with it, he decided, left it there and walked downstairs, mindful of his head.

Girls were busy behind the front desk. One at the switchboard, another sorting mail. The blonde one who had signed him in, saw him and smiled.

She lifted his card. "You didn't put down how long you would be staying with us, Mr. Stanwood."

Stanwood rubbed his jaw. "I can't say exactly. I mean, it all depends, miss."

"Shall we say for a few days, then? Three or four. We have to honour previous reservations, you see."

"I suppose three or four would be all right," Stanwood conceded. "I'm down here looking for somebody, and she might have moved on."

The girl cocked her head. "Oh?"

Stanwood took a worn envelope from his pocket. He held it far from his eyes, squinting to see the return address.

"Cedar View Burrow, Rosslare Strand," he read. "It's the last local address we had from her." He handed the envelope to the girl. "There was one more recently where she was working, in Dublin. But I missed her there. They thought perhaps she might have come back to Rosslare. It's a small town. Perhaps you know the family here.''

She was staring curiously at him. "Would that be Noreen Kelly that you're looking for, then?''

Stanwood nodded, brightening. "Yes. Do you know her?''

She had turned away. Now she laughed, calling, "Noreen?''

Next to the cashier's office, a door opened. A young girl came out, pushing her arms into a short coat. Stanwood stared at her glowing red hair. She was putting a brown scarf over it. His jaw dropped, and he blinked. It's Kate, all over again, he thought.

The blonde girl waved the envelope. "This gentleman is Mr. Stanwood. He's come to see about a girl called Noreen Kelly of Rosslare Strand.''

The redhead stopped short. She paled, then looked at him and shrieked. "Bill – Bill Stanwood! Oh, my God!''

She came running out from behind the desk counter, and threw herself at him. Incredible, Stanwood thought, she's off her feet. He braced to hold her. Thin arms were wrapped tightly around his neck. She was kissing him, and he could feel her heart beating wildly through her open coat. Her lips moved over his face, and then were at his ear. She was babbling incoherent words, crying.

He put her down gently, holding her shoulders. "It was Kate's wish that I see you. Up till the end, she was hoping –''

She burst into fresh tears, stamping her booted foot. "Oh, my dear, poor Kate. I'm so sorry, Bill. I couldn't, I just never could get away. You understand, don't you? But I can't blame you for hating me. My own sister! Was she ill for long before it took her, Bill?''

He had to stay clear of her questions or he would be lost again. There were things he had to say, certainly, but knowing he was on perilous ground, he wanted to go at it slowly, at his own guided pace.

He tried to smile reassuringly, shaken by her uncanny resemblance to Kate. "It's all right, Noreen. Katie knew you'd be there if you could. I've lots to tell you, many things she wanted you to hear about."

"Oh, Bill," she wailed. "How ever did you find me?"

Before he could answer, he saw her attention gone, her expression change. She seemed to be looking somewhere above his head, as if in sudden thought. Her bright, sapphire eyes dilated, her lips twisted. There was a sharp intake of breath, and then she recovered. A horn was honking insistently outside.

She shook her head impatiently. Her voice became shrill, the words poured out with glib urgency. "Oh, Bill, I'm sorry. Somebody is waiting for me. Can I see you another time – later, perhaps?"

He nodded vigorously. "No problem. I'll be here a few days, and we'll have all the time to – "

She threw herself at him again, hugging him tightly, her face smothered in his chest. Then she broke away and ran down the red-carpeted hall. A small yellow car was parked outside the front glass doors. He saw the quick flash of her legs, the door slammed shut, and the car sped off. A pale youth with light hair was behind the wheel.

The reservation girl was speaking. "Well, and aren't you the luckiest man! Would you ever in your right mind have thought it would be so easy to find your Noreen Kelly?"

Stanwood was shaking his head. No, ma'am, he wanted to say, not in a million years! But he did not respond, and walked trance-like toward the front glass doors.

Was he wrong about Noreen's expression, the subtle change before she ran off?

He stood staring out through the glass, hearing the voices of guests conversing pleasantly behind him. His shoulders were hunched. He looked down and saw his fists clenched. Come on, man, he told himself, you imagined it.

He shook his head imperceptibly, stubbornly. How could he have imagined it? And how could he be mistaken, when he had seen that same frozen mask of terror hundreds of times over the years? A detective of homicide can be wrong about many things. But early on, if he is to survive, he learns to recognize the scent of fear, and its accompanying look. He lives by that talent, or dies for the lack of it.

He stood there, rigid, staring outward, his gnarled thick fingers rubbing the battered smooth knuckles.

What the devil was she afraid of?

Now Katie, my dear, he was saying inside himself, it's nothing to worry about. Whatever it is, I'll see to it, and make it come right.

A gust of wind whipped up a fresh flurry of rain. It covered the glass and Stanwood turned away, nodding, talking silently to himself.

Three

Later in his room, his circling thoughts nagged without resolution. Did I see the fear or imagine it? Did she change colour or not? What was that about? Was it me reminding her of Kate, knocking her off-centre somehow? Why did I frighten her so? And if not me, then who else? Nobody was around.

Stanwood could think of no answers. The orbiting questions hovered inside the far corners of his mind, distant and beyond his understanding. He realized he knew nothing of this younger sister. The few words she had babbled in his ear were no more than normal feelings of guilt for having neglected Kate. The frozen look of fright or terror that had suddenly seized her, he decided, had to be an alien feeling. Nothing to do with him.

The rain had stopped. Sunlight reflected off the trees and shimmering roofs. He thought if he took a walk and saw something of the village, it might help. Clarify his thinking, get him off this morbid, convoluted track that led nowhere.

His clothes in the warming room were dry. His hat was a tighter fit. Too much of a good thing there. Wearing a sweater under his coat, he went down the angled staircase.

Guests sat along the corridors, or strolled. There were side rooms for cards, music, writing. A large TV room. The long bar at the north front was well-stocked, crowded at half-day. Behind it was a games room used for snooker.

The long, carpeted corridor led to the east wing with a smaller bar and serving counter. Pretty young girls in their green dress uniforms were offering sweets, tea and coffee. Outside the walled glass windows and rear door was a flagged terrace. Gulls screeched when he stepped out, and he heard the surf below the windbreak bluff.

Cars were parked closely together in front of the hotel entrance. A large lot across the street held more. He crossed to the single sidewalk running there, and walked north along the main street. An occasional small car sped by, tyres humming on the narrow, wet road.

This main street, it appeared, was all there was to it. A few separated houses and stores. No compact village, as such. Chemist', grocery and meat market. Antique shop across the road. Old brick house with a Bed and Breakfast sign in the window. Along the grassy stretch near the water, there were clusters of white huts. Caravans. Not much to the town, he thought.

He passed a church. Across from it was a school. High treble voices of children were singing in hymnlike chorus.

It was Thursday afternoon in Rosslare and Stanwood felt the oddity of being a stranger. He tried to get the feeling of Kate growing up here. She had given off nothing of this small place.

The next crossing was flooded, and he circled the big puddle in its centre. He heard a car coming up behind him. It passed on his right, too close, and the splash of water surprised him. He had forgotten drivers in Ireland used the left lane with their right-hand drive vehicles. He shook himself off. Wake up, he berated himself, things are different here.

He continued walking, and his mind switched again to Noreen. If he was to interpret the look of fear and surprise passing so quickly over her face, he would have to sum up what little he knew of her life.

Kate was still comparatively young when she had died the past year Christmas week. Noreen, he estimated, could be near 25 now, a little child when Kate had left Rosslare for good. During the years Noreen grew up, Katie was lavish with presents. Blouses, shoes, stockings, whatever caught her eye for the younger sister.

Then, abruptly, Noreen's letters stopped coming. Kate continued writing to the old place in Rosslare, despite the lack of response. One day Noreen wrote. She had been away from home, had visited briefly, and was going away again. There was a job in Dublin. This note carried the Rosslare address, and was in the envelope Stanwood held. There was a card from Belfast, then the following year a letter from the Dublin hotel where she was working. She was doing well, she wrote, and hoped Kate was well. Kate was dying, instead, from a malignant tumourous growth.

When Stanwood reached Dublin, he had spent three days searching for Noreen Kelly. She had left her last employment for another hotel. She then worked as a cashier at a coffee shop. She left there to work briefly in a bank as a teller. A girl in the bank manager's office told Stanwood she had moved up north to Belfast. No forwarding address. Discouraged, he had returned to his Dublin hotel. A girl working the night shift at Reservations remembered Noreen having worked with her recently. She believed Noreen had returned to Rosslare. And so Stanwood had taken the next morning train down.

He had not thought of asking personal questions about Noreen of her employers, nor had any comments been offered of her character or diligence. He wanted only to see the girl, pass on Kate's wedding ring, for luck, as Kate had wanted, let her have some of the early photos of Kate, offer financial help if it was needed.

Stanwood stopped. The road curved away at this point and had lost its sidewalk. He faced a sign at a gatepost. ROSSLARE GOLF CLUB. He walked up the long gravel driveway. A sign directed him to the pro shop at the rear. But at the front there were lighted windows. Men were inside drinking at the bar, playing snooker. He walked in, ordered a beer, a glass of Irish Harp, and took it to a table at the side.

The golfers were playful, and in high spirits. They were a garrulous lot, but contrary to their custom of

conviviality, none approached Stanwood. His distant
brooding air permitted no contact. From time to time,
their eyes shifted to him, as if concerned for the man.

Because Stanwood was fundamentally easy-going
and sentimental, he thought himself genial. Perhaps he
was, talking to young children, or when helping old
ladies get their act and groceries together. But there
was a no-nonsense look about him, and when
combined with his rugged features and powerful build,
he presented a formidable appearance. Years on the
force had cemented the set of his stolid face,
commanding a homicide detective squad had solidified
the instinctive manner of authority, and in short, the
man was never mistaken for Santa Claus.

His concentration had been broken when his wife
died, and with his purpose and direction blunted, he
became less brusque and direct, seemingly aimless in
his manner. But the smouldering power remained
somewhere behind his eyes.

His mind had switched back to Noreen. You have to
remember, he reminded himself, that if she has a
problem, it's hers and not your business. She's Katie's
sister but a stranger, just the same. And if she's
borrowed trouble and wants your help, she's old
enough now to ask for it.

Just the same, he thought doggedly, I'd like to know
what scared her so. Was it the sound of the horn, the
boy she was meeting outside? Something about me,
which reminded her all of a sudden I'm a cop? She
may not know I've given it all up.

He got himself another beer. The golfers watched
him from their distance. He cast a pall on their fun,
though, and they were relieved when he left. He walked
slowly back to the hotel annoyed with himself for
seeing only the worst of it.

Four

He looked impatiently at the clock, and asked the girl behind the desk when Noreen would be returning to work.

"I don't know, sir. Perhaps later tonight, but I can't be sure. She works part-time, you see. Special hours."

"Special hours?"

"Yes, sir."

"If she doesn't work tonight, do you think she would be working tomorrow?"

"Tomorrow? That would be Friday. I'm not certain, sir. If not, then she would most likely be in Monday."

"Her work – what does she do here?"

"A little of everything, like the rest of us. But mostly, Noreen works inside the office."

"The office?"

The girl raised her thumb over her shoulder. "Cashier's office. Does she know you're staying here, sir?"

"Yes. I spoke to her earlier, as she was leaving."

Her smile was meant to be comforting. "Then she'll know where to get in touch with you, sir, now wouldn't she?"

"I suppose so."

He turned away. There was a glossy plastic bulletin board on the near wall. Daily activities had been chalked in. After dinner, there was to be a fashion show. Later, dancing with music from Tim Herrick and his Wexford Five. Names were being taken for Scotch foursomes. Prizes offered for low scores.

Stanwood was impatiently moving away when he

saw two other notices. Rosslare Golf Club was hosting an international match on Saturday and Sunday for charity. Prominent Irish and English celebrities were expected to attend.

The second notice was decorated with fanciful drawings in colour of witches riding broomsticks, dancing around black cauldrons, along with huge black cats and pumpkins. ALL-HALLOWS EVE COSTUME BALL, it read. Friday 9 p.m. OCT. 31st. Prizes were to be awarded for the best costumes.

Stanwood had lost track of time and ordinary events. He was surprised to learn the next night was Hallowe'en.

He went to the bar and had a drink. He finished it quickly and walked by the desk again. He made a point of having the girl notice him. She gave no indication that Noreen had returned.

He patrolled the long corridors restlessly. When he came to the desk again, the girl shook her blonde head.

"I'll page you, sir, if Noreen comes back."

He nodded. "Will you be working late?"

"Past eight, sir. And I'll leave word with the girl after me."

"You have the name? Stanwood."

"Yes, sir. Would you be the gentleman that's Noreen's uncle?"

"Brother-in-law."

"Oh?" The blue eyes were puzzled, trying to fathom it.

"I married her sister."

"Sure and I didn't know she had one."

Stanwood waved his hand vaguely. "Katherine. Kate Kelly. She left here a long time ago. We were married in the States."

The young girl stared. "Wait, now. I remember my mother telling me. She's a neighbour to Eileen Kelly –

we've known the family for years. You'd be the police officer, then?"

Stanwood nodded. "What's your name, miss?"

"Sheila Nolan. And how is your wife doing, sir?"

Stanwood tried to make it matter of fact. "She died last year. Just after Christmas."

The girl quickly crossed herself. "Saints preserve us! I'm dreadful sorry, sir."

Stanwood shook his head. "I don't understand it. I thought the family knew. Kate wrote many times. I wrote when she died."

The girl sighed. "I couldn't explain, sir. But there've been changes on this side, too. Some time back, Mr. Kelly passed on, too, sir."

"Kate's father?"

"Aye, and Noreen's. You didn't know about that?"

"Not a word. When did he die?"

"Nigh on three years ago, sir. It was his heart gave out."

Stanwood shook his head, disturbed. "They should have told Kate. Somebody should have let her know."

"I know what you're saying, sir. But the family's had its troubles, you see. And Noreen left for good after the new gentleman moved in."

"Three years ago?"

"Before that. She wasn't about to like her new stepfather."

"What's his name?"

"Matt Bogson. He's a big man. About your size, sir."

Stanwood stood still, trying to be patient. "From what you're telling me, is it possible Mrs. Kelly – Kate's mother, doesn't know she died?"

The girl answered quickly. "Oh, no, sir, it's not that. I believe she knew. What I'm trying to say is, she didn't want to know. Perhaps you'll be seeing her while you're here, and then you'll understand better."

Stanwood shrugged. "I hope I do. I'll wait to see Noreen first, and then pay my respects."

"Yes, sir. Noreen can explain it all to you far better than I. It's the Kelly family to its own doings, after all."

She'll have to do a lot of explaining to manage that, Stanwood thought. Maybe it's the strange family that drove Kate away in the first place.

The telephone rang and the girl picked it off the counter. She listened a moment. "No, she's not here. She may be back later tonight, but I'm not certain. I believe she's off."

That would be for Noreen, Stanwood thought. Apparently he wasn't the only one wanting to see her. He couldn't very well ask the girl who was calling.

She had hung up without taking down any message. Now she turned to look at the antique clock on the wall. Stanwood was starting off. "Mr. Stanwood," she said, "they'll be starting to serve dinner at half-seven."

"Half-seven?" They had their own ways of speaking here. "Thanks," he said. "Guess I'll go up and change."

He approached the top of the first landing warily, careful of his head and the low abutment. A woman was coming down the steps above him. She stopped short at the angled landing and peered down over the banister. Stanwood looked at her as she hung over the rail.

She smiled. "I never know what time it is." He stared blankly. He was about to give her the time from his wrist-watch, when she drew back, nodding. "Oh, I see it now. Nearly six." Aware of his puzzled look, she pointed down. "It's in the glass there. But backward. You just turn it around."

She scampered back up the steps, and disappeared from view down the hallway. Stanwood, about to

continue on his way, stopped suddenly. He stepped to
the railing, peering down and around, as she had.

He noticed for the first time the small circular
mirror tilted on the wall of the reservation desk area.
At this angle, it reflected the old clock on the side wall
behind the desk.

That's a new one, Stanwood thought. Saves the
switchboard girl the trouble of reading off the time to
the guests.

Wait a moment, he thought, there's your solution.
He walked down the steps of the first landing again to
the main floor. He was trying to remember exactly
where he had been standing with Noreen.

He found the approximate spot, looked over his
shoulder and saw the mirror high on the wall. Then he
stepped to the place she had been standing facing him.
He let his knees sag, lowering his eye level about a foot.
He swore silently.

She had been looking at him, and then her eyes
shifted over his shoulder. Lost in a new thought, he
had assumed, then afraid somehow. Now he knew it
need be nothing like that. It didn't have to be that way
at all.

From her position, it was evident, the mirror would
have reflected the image of any person standing on the
first landing. Looking down at her, perhaps,
deliberately, or somebody she had, in that quick
instant, seen in the glass.

Seen and recognized. Somebody whose presence she
did not expect. Not anticipate, as well? Perhaps, he
thought, pursuing his reconstruction of that elusive
moment when Noreen had shifted her eyes away, and
radiated terror.

Somebody from out of the past, or possibly the
present. In any event, a danger to her, a threat renewed
or as yet unfulfilled.

He shifted positions, unconscious of guests strolling by, doggedly replaying the scene earlier in the day. Well, what could it be? Who was it that posed the threat?

Stanwood rubbed his knuckles. She'll want to be telling me who it was, he thought, and why he scared the wits out of her.

He was nodding his head, hunching his shoulders, lips silently moving along with his thoughts, when suddenly he had a bitter realization of his true position here.

Her life is none of your affair, he reproached himself. And you gave up playing at being a detective six months ago. The girl can live her own life without you interfering.

He broke off immediately with his uneasy thoughts, and went back up the stairs to his room, this time without incident.

Five

He noticed he was the only one remaining in the bar. The guests apparently took their dining seriously. He went forward into the hotel restaurant. It was spacious and comfortable. Over a hundred tables and seemingly all were occupied. The hum of conversation and tinkling of glass filled the room.

The headwaiter was approaching, dressed formally. "My name is Stanwood," he said. "I'm expecting a call."

The headwaiter nodded. "Will you be staying with us long?"

"A few days."

He followed the man past empty tables. The

headwaiter flicked a hand indicating small blue cards on the white cloth. "Those are reserved, sir. I'll have to find you your own table."

He looked around. "Everybody seems to be in. Any table will do."

"It's not allowed, sir. They may still pop in. People come here for the same week year after year. They'll expect their own table. You're by yourself, sir? Here's one at the side."

The menu was extensive and varied, the food excellent. Little girls in the green uniform came by, serving vegetables, going from table to table about the large dining-room like well organized troops. There was never a lull in the humming conversation all around him. The Irish and their gift of gab, he thought, wryly wishing he could be part of it.

The guests were well dressed. It was a poor country but they didn't reflect it. The small cars parked outside had no bearing on it. The headwaiter was walking by and he signalled him over.

"Everything all right, sir?"

"Fine. You said your guests come back here year after year at the same time. Why is that?"

"They like the place, sir. And they've met people they like, and taken to. They all reserve when they leave to come back the following year on the same date."

Stanwood shifted his eyes. He saw smiles and animation at every table. "Why in Rosslare? Anything special here?"

"Nothing really, sir. There's the beach along back there. And the air is fine. Wexford town is not far off. There's the golf links down the road. I think they like the hotel itself, sir. The food and the service, the staff. It's like one big happy family here, sir."

After dinner, he strolled the long corridors. Guests were congregating in the lounge area at the rear. There was a ballroom, platform for an orchestra. The girls in green at the service counter were obliging filling demi-tasse cups or pouring tea. There were still flurries of rain against the wide expanse of windows. Nobody would be walking the dark strand of beach, taking the Rosslare air.

He walked to the front desk again. A new girl was sorting out papers. "My name is Stanwood. Room 26. Any calls for me?"

She looked up blankly. "Calls, sir?"

He waved his hands, an edge to his voice. "The other girl said she would leave word – "

She looked down at a note pad. "Oh, yes, Sheila told me to watch out for you, when she left. You'll be the man from the States?"

He nodded. "Do you know Noreen Kelly?"

"That I wouldn't sir. I'm new here. I can leave word – "

He was turning away. "It's all right. I'll be in my room if she calls."

Stanwood kept his ears open and alert all that evening for the phone to ring, but all he heard was the continuing soft rain, sudden violent gusts of wind shaking the windows.

Six

He woke early Friday to clear skies. The morning wind was gentle, riffling the tall trees across the hotel grounds, blowing soft ripples on the sea.

A new girl was behind the desk. He asked if Noreen had come in. "I don't believe so, sir. But then Friday is usually her day off, you know."

He watched her sorting newspapers, marking them with guest room-numbers. "Can I buy one of those?"

"I'll be happy to have them delivered to your room each day, sir."

"Fine. I'm Stanwood. Room 26." He picked up the *Irish Times*. "What do I pay you for this?"

"Fifteen pence, sir."

He sorted out the Eire coins, beginning to get the hang of it. "What time is breakfast?"

"Half-eight, sir. If you're needing coffee or tea, meanwhile, you can get it around the rear lounge."

He was one of the few early risers. The frail little girl in green at the service counter smiled up at him. "Good morning, sir. Will it be coffee or tea you're wanting?"

He took his coffee around to the red-carpeted corridor with its great length of glass providing a complete view of the hotel grounds and the hedged windbreak to the sea. The early morning sun was warming. He took a reclining chair, had his coffee, and read the Dublin newspaper.

The headlines were black and stark. Petrol strike spreading, economy moves threatening employment, tragedy of an IRA bomb blast in a London hotel killing six people, injuring several others. There was a picture showing the debris of the bomb, the victims sprawled inertly among shattered glass and collapsed beams.

Stanwood closed his paper and stared out the window. He had lived close to violence most of his life, and had never yet understood the mind of the assassin. The uncaring killer of faceless victims; random murder by proxy was strange to him.

Later, when he went in for breakfast, he was unable to respond to the cheerful greeting of the headwaiter. The man wore a name tag on his jacket woven in green thread: Dennis Doyle.

Stanwood folded his paper to the side as the waiter poured coffee. "Terrible news this morning, sir. You've already read it, have you?"

Stanwood nodded. "I've read it. And read of it before while in the States. I don't understand it. How can they be proud of something like this?"

"Well, sir, that would be the work of the revolutionary party, the IRA Provos. Not all Ulster is behind the killing, you know."

Stanwood opened the paper, pointing to the photo. "These are all innocent people. Nothing to do with your political war. Doesn't something like this reflect on all you Irish?"

"We regret it, sir, but we don't see it that way. The people in Northern Ireland aren't in agreement with it all either, you see. It's a poor place they have there, and when they come down to Dublin, or here, there's no hard feeling. We got tired of the fighting, you see, but they're still going on with it."

Stanwood looked surprised. "They come down here from Belfast?"

"There's no law against it. We all go back and forth, if there's a need, and everybody's welcome. There's friends and relatives, still. It's just the six counties up north, and Ireland is still mother to us all."

"Anybody down here from Belfast now? I'd sure like to talk to him, get his reasoning on it before I go back home."

"At the hotel, you mean, sir? I can't say for certain. Friday's the day most visitors check in or out. But you might speak to Jerry at the golf club."

"Jerry?"

"The bartender. Big, dark fellow. He's from Belfast."

Stanwood dimly recalled the dour dark-visaged man behind the club bar. There was nothing of the convivial bartender about him. He filled the orders, set the glasses down, and that was the end of it. In his own distant mood, he hadn't offered any conversation. Perhaps later he would try to get the hang of the political question. Meanwhile, he hated all terrorists on general principles.

The question now was what to do with his day. Noreen had said she would get back to him. He had to remind himself that the girl had a life of her own, and his sudden presence could not be expected to change or shape it in any way. He considered now what he would say to her about Kate, to ease the guilt he had seen in her eyes. After they had their conversation, he would decide whether or not to see her mother. Perhaps she would want to know a little more about the daughter she had not seen or written to for so many years.

After breakfast, guests were reclining in the sunning chairs outside on the stone terrace. With the prospect of a good day, they were out in force. "Sure, and it's a fine day, is it not?" "Aye, and it is." Stanwood smiled at the lilting Irish tongue.

Outside the sunning area, a small bluff covered by a thick-hedged windbreak led down a few steps to the sand and sea. The water sparkled green and hazy in the distance. He walked close to the spindrift along the shore. The damp sand was covered with a multitude of small shells and coloured stones.

A glittering brilliant light blinded his vision. He saw the curving strand ending not far off to his right. A lighthouse was angled beyond on a huge rock promontory reflecting the morning sun. He turned with the sea on his right and walked north, his feet sinking into the crusted thin surface of sand. Ahead the strand curved gently, crescentlike towards a grassy headland he thought bordered the golf course.

The air was wonderfully clean, and Stanwood lifted his broad chest and breathed deeply. There was a tangy sweet quality to this air, something to be savoured. He had been to the beaches in Los Angeles but it was not the same. This was a revelation, to encounter really pure air. Now, with nothing to do in his life, with nothing to look forward to, he thought perhaps after this visit, he might want to return to Ireland and Rosslare.

The people are fine, the food is good, and the air can't be beat, he told himself. What more would a man want?

He looked at the sky, the scudding fleecy clouds, and remembered the daily downpour in Dublin. Rosslare, someone had said, didn't catch as much. Well, he thought, if that's a fact, and it's nearly always like it is today, maybe I'll be back.

Seven

When he returned to the hotel after his walk, Sheila, the shapely blonde behind the check-in desk called to him.

"You've had a phone call, Mr. Stanwood."

He hurried over. "Was it Noreen?"

"I don't know, sir. Another girl took the call. Here's the message."

She handed him a small slip of paper. The note read: MEET YOU IN CULLIMORE'S TAVERN IN WEXFORD AT FOUR.

"Where's Wexford?"

"A small town about ten miles from here, sir."

He showed her the note. "This tavern – is it hard to find?"

She read, smiling. "Oh, Tim Cullimore's will be no problem, sir. It's just off the quay at the centre of town. You go up Oyster Lane to Distillery Road. That would be two blocks off the water." She glanced at the clock. "It's only the morning. You'll have plenty of time."

"Ten miles," Stanwood said. "I don't have a car. Can one be rented here? Or can I get a taxi?"

She shook her head. "No cars for hire here, sir, nor taxis. Wexford town's the place for that."

"Damn. How'll I get there?"

"Well, there's a train – " She glanced at the clock. "No, I'm afraid you've just missed that. There's not another until late this evening."

"All I need is a lift there. Noreen could drive me back. She has a car, hasn't she?"

Her eyebrows lifted. "Oh, then it's Noreen you're meeting?"

He frowned, looking at the note. "Who else? She's the only one in this neck of the woods knows I'm here."

"Just a moment, Mr. Stanwood. I'll ask the girl at the switchboard. If she spoke to Noreen, perhaps there's more."

Stanwood waited impatiently as she walked across the room to the switchboard at the rear. She was showing the note to the girl seated there. The switchboard girl was shaking her head.

"I'm sorry, sir," the blonde girl said, "but Angela's new here. She doesn't know Noreen's voice. There wasn't anything else said, so she says, about driving you back here."

"Well, naturally – "

"But if it was Noreen, if she doesn't have her car with her, she can get you a lift back. That or find you a taxi."

Stanwood rubbed his hands. "Fine. Then all I need

is a way to get there. Ten miles, you say? Not too much of a walk, but still – " He broke off, staring at something glittering in her hand.

"You can take my car. It's Hallowe'en tonight. I'll not be leaving until late." She dropped the keys on the counter. "It's the little black Fiat across the lot. A bit crowded for you, but it'll get you there fine."

Stanwood's fingers curled over the car keys and then drew away. "Awfully kind of you, Sheila. But I don't know how long I'll be with Noreen. We've a lot to talk about. I wouldn't want to put you out."

She shrugged. "Well, it will be time for lunch soon. You might ask Dennis. He might know somebody from here driving into Wexford later. Lots of them do. There's not much doing around Rosslare."

"Dennis?"

"The head waiter, sir."

Stanwood remembered the label on the young maitre-d's coat. "Oh, Doyle?"

"Yes, sir. Or he might be off after lunch himself, and take you there."

"Well, that's awfully nice – "

"Dennis got himself married recently," she said smiling. "He lives not far from Wexford. And he's still in the habit of dropping by afternoons. To see how things are, you understand."

Stanwood grinned. "Sure. Not a bad idea. Keep the honeymoon going."

"At any rate," the girl said, "you'll have no problem. If Dennis can't arrange it for you, my offer stands. My little car has been to Wexford and back so many times, it can get you there blindfolded."

"Well, I may have to take you up on that," Stanwood said. "But I'll talk to Doyle and see what he has to say about it."

It was a little after noon when he went up to Dennis

Doyle before seating himself at his table. Doyle clucked sympathetically at his problem.

"Sheila's car is too small for you, man. You'll suffocate yourself in that little mite."

"Well, perhaps, but there's the other matter. I don't know how long I'll be, and I wouldn't want to keep her waiting after work. The same goes for you, too. I'd just as soon hire a taxi both ways, if I could get one."

Doyle looked closely at him. "That'd be expensive, man. Paddy would have to come all the way out here to get you."

"Paddy?"

"Paddy Moran. Friend of mine who runs a taxi service."

"Can you get him? I've got to be there at four."

"Then you'll not be minding the price? It could run you five pounds each way."

Stanwood shook his head firmly. "Believe me, that's no problem. I'll feel freer about it, and not be obligated to you or Sheila."

"Then I'll call him for you. You can start your lunch in the meantime, and I'll be back to you."

Stanwood had just finished the first course, a light fish soup, when the headwaiter returned.

"You're all set, sir. Paddy will be here by three. It's a short ride, and give you some time to look around, see Wexford."

"Fine. Much obliged."

"Have you decided on your main course now?"

Stanwood nodded, feeling relieved, grateful for Noreen's message. "I think I'd like to hold that off for a bit, and have a big glass of Scotch, if you can handle that."

"No problem, sir. And you'll be the one has to handle it."

Stanwood grinned back at him. Things were looking

up. He sat back, feeling younger, more alive. If Kate could only see me now, he thought, know where I'm going, she'd get a big kick out of it.

Eight

Stanwood was pacing outside the Strand Hotel, glancing at his watch, when the ancient taxi of Paddy Moran turned in the drive. It was a Rover, a classic in its day. Now it was just a late cab.

"Sure and you wouldn't be the gentleman going to Wexford?"

"Doyle said you'd be here at three. It's nearer three-thirty."

The driver was short and chunky, wearing an old battered cap. "Aye, that I am. But then Doyle never told the little imps in Wexford town not to soap up me windshield while I was having a glass at McSwiney's bar."

Stanwood settled in the back seat and Moran eased out of the driveway. "Why would they do that?"

"Because the little buggers can't wait to be playin' their tricks. It's All-Hallows this evening, you know."

"Hallowe'en? I forgot. I've got to be at Cullimore's by four. Think you'll make it?"

"Tim Cullimore's? With time to spare, sir." He caught Stanwood's eye in the rear-view mirror. "And did my friend Doyle give you a price for the ride there?"

"That's no problem. Whatever you say. I may need a ride back, too. In fact, if you have the time, you can consider yourself hired for the next few hours."

"I know you're from the States," Moran said. "But

even so, man, it will cost you a few pounds."

"Okay. It's worth it." He patted the worn leather seat. "This is the first decent-size car I've seen since getting here."

"Aye, the Rover was built for the likes of you." Moran spat tobacco juice derisively out his window. "Can't stand these pesky little bug types myself. They ain't proper cars to be riding in. More like toys. Built for the women and children."

"Right on, brother," Stanwood said, smiling.

The old car cruised smoothly, its powerful engine purring a deep, throaty growl. They were on a main highway. The hills were yellow and green. The houses were far apart, interspersed with farms. "What do they farm here?"

"Dairy, mostly. We've the best in butter and cream. That's to say, outside of what's best in your glass of the stuff." Stanwood was nodding contentedly. Damn nice and peaceful here. You can relax, get some decent air in your lungs. The voice of the cabbie broke into his thoughts. "If you don't mind my asking, sir, is it business brought you down here?"

"Kind of. Personal business. Why?"

"You've the look of a copper. After some poor devil now, are you not, sir?"

Stanwood chuckled. "I may still have the look, Paddy, but not the job. I quit. Retired. Let somebody else do the chasing."

"Got the pension then, have you not?"

"You bet. Did my twenty-five years."

"Good for you, sir. Now if I may ask, what brought you down to Rosslare?"

Normally taciturn, Stanwood felt relaxed and at ease with the bantering cabbie. Well, what have I got to hide? he thought, and told Moran about Kate. "It's her younger sister I'm meeting at Cullimore's. I just had a moment with her when I arrived at the hotel. Once I get to sit down with her and talk, I'll feel I've accomplished something."

"I'm thinking it will be good for the young one, too. Hearing how it went with her sister. Before the trouble, as well."

Ahead was a wide expanse of water cluttered with ships. Beyond, rising on a hill, Stanwood could make out a village.

"There's Wexford town, and here's our River Slaney. You'll make your appointment with time to spare."

He turned against heavy oncoming traffic into a narrow street. Shops lined both sides. The car filled most of the lane. The walk was too narrow for pedestrians and they were all over the street. They gave ground grudgingly. Children ran around yelling, wearing Hallowe'en costumes.

Moran indicated the tourists blocking his passage. "When they built this town, there were no cars at all, and they never did get around to make driving easier."

The village was old and quaint, Stanwood thought, the kind of place people send postcards from. Most of the streets were too narrow to permit more than one-way traffic.

"In truth," the driver said, "it's the Danes who laid out this place hundreds of years ago, when they first come over. They built it small and tight the better to fight out of. And then the Normans took it, but only after the commander burned his ships and his troops had to fight to win it over."

Stanwood, looking out, knew he was on historic ground, but now his mind had switched to the meeting with Noreen, and he had lost his patience for historic love within the past few minutes.

"How much longer till we get there?" he said.

The driver had been driving slowly and cautiously, waiting for the pedestrians to move along, advancing inch by inch. Now he stopped on the crowded narrow street and flicked his thumb out the window.

"Here you are, sir. Just outside your door is Cullimore's Tavern."

Stanwood glanced again at his watch. He was early by ten minutes. He reached into his pocket, peeling pound notes off the thick roll. "I may need you later, Paddy, but I don't know yet if the girl has her car to take me back with her. Suppose you check here in an hour, and tell me now if this is good enough to hold you."

Moran grinned, riffling the bills. "Sure and you're a generous man. This will more than do for the ride and back, not to mention the day after."

"See you about five, then."

Nine

The tavern was old, so quiet he felt it as a cloister with a religious hush to it, after the din outside. There was a darts room in the rear with targets and blackboard, small round tables, benches and chairs. High on the wall were old swords, dirks and daggers, Gaelic shields and plaques. Fastened to the ceiling were old-fashioned wooden fans. There were framed pictures along the walls and behind the long wooden bar. A few patrons sat conversing softly with the bartender.

His eyes adjusted quickly to the lighting and he saw Noreen was not there. He glanced at his watch. He was early. He ordered a drink at the bar and took it to a wooden-backed booth facing the door. Maybe I'll catch her expression and mood before she sees me, he thought. If anything is wrong, I'll know it before the glad smile comes on.

A few men came in, joining the group at the bar. Their laughter and camaraderie was low key. Glasses tinkled. It was a restful place. After twenty minutes, he went to the bar for another. The bartender walked over briskly, smiling.

"Are you Tim Cullimore?"

The bartender was pale with a dented nose, bushy eyebrows, husky, dark-eyed. "Aye, that I am."

Stanwood noted the sloping shoulders, big hands, marked face. Perhaps he had been a fighter in his prime twenty years back. "Would you know Noreen Kelly?"

There was a quick flicker in the man's eyes. Now he was appraising Stanwood.

"And who wants to know?" he asked, still smiling.

"I'm her brother-in-law – from the States. She was supposed to meet me here at four. My name is Stanwood. Perhaps she called and left a message."

Cullimore shook his head. "I'm sorry, sir, but she hasn't. Yes, I know Noreen. If she told you she'd be here at four, you'll have to believe her, man." His brown eyes looked Stanwood over. "Brother-in-law, did you say?"

Stanwood shrugged. "Married her sister Kate. She left Ireland years ago."

"Aye, I've heard tell. Pleased to meet you, Mr. Stanwood, and would you be having a drink on the house, sir?"

Stanwood watched Cullimore pour the drink. "Thanks. How well do you know Noreen?"

Again, Stanwood felt the instinctive cautious shift in the man's eyes. "That's not for me to say, sir. She'll tell you whatever you want to know about that, sir, when you're talking to her."

Stanwood walked back to the booth. He kept his eyes on the street. An occasional customer came in. Children were screaming, swooping down the street, yelling in the open door. Some had their faces painted, others wore hideous masks, goblin outfits, masks of apes, monsters. Stanwood was trying to remember himself as a child playing Hallowe'en pranks on the neighbours. "Trick or treat!"

He finished his drink and returned to the bar. "One more of the same." He placed a few Irish pounds on the bar.

Cullimore drew his drink and pushed the green notes back. "Till your next visit with us, I'm not charging you, man."

Stanwood glanced at his watch. "Hey, be reasonable. I might be waiting here all night."

"She said she'd be, no? Give the girl time."

Stanwood felt awkward picking up his money. "You don't have to do this. I'm happy to pay."

"Not at Tim Cullimore's, you don't. Go back there and enjoy your drink. I'll keep me eye on the door for you."

The bar stools soon were all occupied. Stanwood sat alone nursing his drink. He saw the battered cap edge through the doorway, and then the cab driver entered. He looked across the room at Stanwood.

"She ain't come by yet?"

Stanwood shook his head.

"You said to come back in the hour."

"I know. Thanks. Make it a half next time." As the cabbie touched his cap and turned to go, Stanwood asked, "Can I buy you a drink?"

"Not just yet, sir. I've got to keep me mind on me old car while those young buggers are roaming the streets."

"They still at it?"

"At it? They ain't hardly begun yet. I'm hoping to be off the streets and home before the night."

The cabbie who had kept one eye on the street, one foot across the threshhold, suddenly wheeled and catapulted himself outward, waving his arms, roaring. "Get off that car, or I'll take my stick to ye."

Stanwood sat restlessly staring across the room. The pub had filled up now, the tomblike silence was gone, and the small room rocked with talk and laughter. The tables about him were occupied. The owner was busy pouring drinks for the crowd around the bar.

Well, we'll give her the extra half hour, Stanwood thought morosely, and if she's not here, I'll take the cab back to the hotel.

Customers kept coming. Paddy Moran came in again. "No luck," Stanwood said, "she hasn't come. I'll be right with you, Paddy."

He shouldered his way through the drinkers. They looked at him tolerantly.

"The man needs a drink bad, Tim. Give it yer best."

"Aye, from the look in his eye, it better be a double."

When he reached the rail, he motioned Cullimore closer. "If she calls, I'll be back at the Rosslare hotel."

"Sorry the girl didn't make it, sir. I'll give her your message."

"It's important."

"Aye. Hope you can drop in on us again during your stay in County Wexford."

"You bet." He backed out, murmuring his apologies. Outside, he looked for Moran and found him in front of his car half-surrounded by a taunting group of children. It appeared as if the Hallowe'en play-acting was past, and violence threatened.

Stanwood parted the half-circle. "Here, you kids, take it easy."

The ringleader turned to defy him, but Stanwood had now assumed his formidable air of strength and authority. The boy stepped back. He spoke to the others. "Well, come on, then, we're not big enough to fight the copper."

They stared up at him through their masks and painted faces. Then without a word, they suddenly broke off and ran clattering down the street.

Moran appeared shaken. "I'll tell ye something, mister. That wasn't all fun and games, now, was it? I mean, that's an ugly lot there."

Stanwood nodding, stepped inside. "Kids," he said.

Ten

As Paddy Moran carefully threaded his big Rover through narrow streets built for dry carts and donkeys, or, farther back still, Danes putting to the sword adventurous Normans, he carried on a one-way conversation, pointing out to his passenger the landmarks and history of the place, going all the way back to the original Fir Bolgs, resuming the travelogue where he had left off when he deposited Stanwood at Cullimore's.

Stanwood heard it all with half an ear, his mind elsewhere, seeing but not seeing, letting the cabbie drone and chortle on while his nagging mind kept repeating over and again, Well, where the hell was she? And why drag me all the way out if she wasn't going to keep the appointment?

Moran, on his own, a happy Irishman with no telepathic gifts shunted accounts of antiquity aside and said, "Then why would the girl call you to set a time and not show herself?"

Stanwood, startled by this remarkable insight into his own stalled thinking, said reasonably, "I don't know, Paddy. Beats me." He rubbed his jaw and added hopefully, "You wouldn't happen to know the Kelly family, would you?"

"In Rosslare? That I don't, sir. I'm not born local, and been here but the few years. The missus and I come from Donegal."

"What brought you here?"

Moran rubbed his hands. "The foul weather, sir. Me bones don't take kindly to the cold and the rain, along with the snow there. Enough of that I had, along with my Imelda. And while there's no escaping rain in all Ireland, still it happens less down here, and there's more of the sun."

"That's why we live in Los Angeles. Plenty of sun there all year round." And a lot of crazies, too. Let's not forget that.

"Aye, so I've heard. But you've the bad air, too, do you not? The smog, is it?"

"Well, you can't have everything, man." He was surprised to hear himself laughing. You've been wound up about this like a kid on his first date, he told himself. Relax, will you? She'll come round. Remember, you just got here.

Eleven

It was dark when Stanwood returned to the Strand in Rosslare. The old hotel was ablaze with lights, the lobby crowded with new arrivals. He wanted a word with the reception-desk girl in the event that Noreen had called and left a message, but the check-in area was clogged with newcomers and their luggage, and he had to withdraw and wait. He was leaning back against a wall scanning the busy scene abstractedly, when he realized suddenly there were several big men standing quietly aside, alert and on their toes. He looked again, recognizing the type immediately as security people. There was no mistaking the stolid men in their trenchcoats and wary, watchful attitude, and he thought at first there had been some accident in the hotel.

He was standing aside in the narrow corridor near the bulletin board, when his eye caught the hotel listing of hotel activities. There was the announcement of the VIP international golf match scheduled for the weekend, he saw again, and now he looked more closely at the arriving guests.

They were a large convivial group, perhaps an even dozen in all, well-dressed, with the look of comfortable authority. They seemed vaguely familiar, but, he reasoned, perhaps from newspaper photos or TV news he had seen. Judging from the beefed-up security around the hotel lobby, it was his guess these were the VIP golfers, here for the charity tournament, Irish, English, or from whatever country they represented.

Rosslare was a small seaside resort, backwater by most standards, with perhaps a thousand residents, at most. Still, he thought, the match with these celebrities could attract a crowd. He recalled the most recent bombing headline in the morning newspaper, and now, given the circumstances, his trained police mind instantly began to compute the chances for an ugly incident, despite the cordon of guards. If there was to be another murder in the mind of some selected assassin, here were the new targets, or at least some among them, vulnerable during their stay at the hotel, and over the weekend in plain view, as they played the flat, windswept Rosslare golf links.

He noticed the new arrivals were chatting in good spirits, laughing easily, not looking the least concerned. Well, he reminded himself, they've had to live with the bomb and bullet for years, and maybe they've got used to it by now.

He wished he understood more clearly the political picture with its strained antagonisms. He knew the problem was religious, complex, and not readily soluble. Now if Noreen were here with him, no doubt she could explain it all quite easily. His temper exploded inwardly. Well, dammit, where was she, and why hadn't she met him at Cullimore's, as arranged? And what was going on with her anyway?

The double line around the reception desk was still intact. Hotel guests were going in for dinner. There would be time to ask for messages later, he decided, and followed the others into the hotel restaurant.

As he passed inside the door, he had a curious moment of recall, and wondered what had happened to the brief moment of exhilaration he had experienced in Paddy Moran's cab just a little while ago. His laughter had seemed to presage happier times.

Well, he thought shrugging, I've waited this long, I can go it a while longer.

Truly, a drag this man was, with sentiment clogging his lines. Old enough to know better, too. Ah, well, it takes all kinds to make a world.

Twelve

The girl at the desk shook her head. No, sir, very sorry but no message.

It was still fairly early in the evening, not yet nine, and Stanwood considered there was still the possibility the girl would call. Failing that, there was the week-end just coming up. And if she still had not called, she was expected in at work Monday, and so there was nothing to do but wait.

Meanwhile he considered ways of delaying going to his room and perhaps falling asleep. The drinks at Cullimore's in Wexford had been compounded at dinner in the hotel, and he was feeling drowsy.

To rouse himself, he stepped outside. It was a cool and clear night, the wind blowing softly off the sea. Some of the hotel guests made it their ritual to go to the south-east wing lounge for after-dinner coffee. Others were sitting outside on the stone terrace relaxing in the big wooden chairs. Stanwood found one for himself close to the thick hedge serving as a windbreak.

The grounds of the hotel were spacious, lit by overhead lights. There was a tennis court at the far end, a layout of miniature golf with rubber balls on subtly demoniacally designed concrete. A young couple were playing tennis, in shorts, despite the cool air. More people joined up for the miniature golf, waiting in line to get to the first hole. A young woman sat at a white iron table inscribing names, and calling out numbers to the people around her. Stanwood discovered this event was part of the hotel Hallowe'en-planned activities, as earlier contestants filed back posting their scores for prizes.

A tall woman in black evening dress stopped near his chair. "Aren't you going to play?"

Stanwood looked up, flustered. "What? Well, no, I haven't thought about that."

Her laugh was musical, softly controlled. "Pity. You're probably like all the other golfers here. Think this is too easy."

Stanwood shook his head. "No, ma'am. I hadn't thought about it either way. And I'm not a golfer, either, for that matter."

She looked down at him. "Really? Then what on earth are you doing down here in Rosslare?"

Stanwood grinned. "Just a short visit. Travelling, ma'am."

She was moving on, speaking over her shoulder. "Well, if you happen to change your mind – "

"I doubt that, but thanks for the encouragement."

He watched her move gracefully away. Was she a single like himself? he wondered. Perhaps he should have responded more positively, had some fun. Was he going to turn this trip to Ireland into a crusade?

He sat back annoyed with himself, feeling old and wretched. That was a damn nice, fine-looking woman, he told himself, and where were you when it was going on?

He closed his eyes. Was there ever going to be another life for himself, he wondered. Was it possible he was through already, just barely into middle age?

The surf beyond the hedge pounded on the shore. Far off he heard soft music. A band in the hotel for the evening after-dinner dance. He wondered if he should go inside, perhaps find a partner, enjoy the evening.

But he was tired, too full after dinner, he told himself, with too many drinks inside him. Forget it,

Bill. Maybe some other time. He relaxed and gave in to his drowsiness.

He couldn't remember feeling this peaceful and content. The wind was soft on his skin, cool, but pleasant enough. He was nodding off, when he heard a chorus of voices. They were singing a strange chant which seemed to break the harmony of the evening. Something too strident about it. Loud voices, shouts. Cries, too. Jeers and raucous laughter.

Stanwood opened his eyes. His hands, he noticed, were already instinctively tensed. Curious, he looked about.

Costumed figures had invaded the hotel terrace grounds from the open rear driveway. They looked to be children, large and small, wearing sheets, scarves, hobgoblin and elfish dress, masked or with their faces painted beyond recognition. They were chanting a repetitious singsong line.

"Death to the witch! Death to the witch!"

They were dancing, prancing, a long winding line snaking across the hotel lawns, and now Stanwood saw they indeed had a witch amongst them, a small black-robed figure wearing the wide-brimmed black conical hat, and the hideous mask with its great jutting nose and toothless grin, the typical witch incarnate, mythologized and depicted so for centuries.

The witch was trapped, Stanwood saw, inside the moving band, a rope around her waist held by two robed figures behind her. He half-rose from his chair, seeing she was being whipped with a long light rod at the end of every cadence, and was half-trotted, on the run, it appeared from her tormentors.

They were turning her away now. Stanwood got to his feet, disturbed. The witch tried to escape, lurching outside the ring. The rope drew tight, dragging her back. The whip was applied. Stanwood couldn't hear a sound from the victim above the chanting, and took a step forward.

A chuckle from the man seated at his right startled him and he turned. "Looks like they caught her early tonight."

"Aren't they hurting that little girl?" Stanwood asked.

"Not a bit," the man said. "All part of it, you see. It's All-Hallow's Eve, you know."

He looked around. The other guests were smiling, unconcerned.

Stanwood hesitated. Perhaps there was a local custom here he knew nothing about. Despite the assurance of the man, he remembered the scene not too many hours past in the town of Wexford. The menacing ring of children surrounding Paddy Moran, the cabbie. Perhaps they were children, but there was nothing of innocence then, but rather a brutal aggressive mob cruelty.

He looked for the flagellant victim again, but the moving line had swerved and now they were leaving the hotel grounds, herding their victim along. In another moment they had disappeared from view, blocked by the wing of the hotel, and he could hear the sound of the chant diminishing until it could not be heard at all. He was shaking his head, still disturbed, when he thought he heard a mournful cry, a muffled scream, as of an animal in pain, but he could not be sure.

A chill pervaded his big frame, and he shook himself. Would he always be a cop at heart?

He wanted to go after the kids, see for himself what was happening. Instead, he stood rooted, indecisive, a stranger in a foreign land. Reading mysteries and violence into things that perhaps were perfectly natural and harmless here.

Still and all, he thought, they play funny games here, and I don't like the way they go at it.

The contestants were still putting the little wayward red rubber golf ball, exhorting each other to do better. The others sat peacefully on their chairs chatting conversationally, as if nothing had happened. Inside the hotel, Stanwood heard laughter above dance music.

He thought he might still find the woman with the musical voice somewhere along the miniature golf layout. Play the game with her, perhaps go in for a dance later, a drink, some conversation. Nothing wrong with that, is there? he asked himself.

He looked at his watch. It was not yet 10 o'clock, the evening still young. But Stanwood felt old, chilled and frustrated. He turned and walked back to the terrace door, knowing he was going upstairs to bed.

Terrible thing to be depressed so.

Thirteen

Saturday morning, the sky was a brilliant expanse of blue, unmarked by the merest wisp of cloud. Stanwood had slept a troubled night and woke tired and stiff. There was a chill to the room which matched his mood.

Before breakfast, he checked the reception desk. Noreen was not expected in, he was told. There were no messages. He turned away, disappointed. She must have her reasons, he told himself. It could be she feels too guilty about neglecting Kate at the end to want to see me. It's understandable. If she's still avoiding me Monday, I'll take the hint and leave.

As he thought about it, he realized there had never been a solid connection between the sisters. Noreen was still a child when Kate left, and how well could they really have known each other? Actually, it was only a sentimental attachment on Kate's part. One-sided, too, unfortunately. Nothing he could do about that.

Down the corridor, he saw the VIP golfers with their bags and guards heading out the front door toward their cars, dressed casually now for the day.

Doyle, the affable young headwaiter, was off this morning, and Stanwood ordered and ate his breakfast in a hurry. The only golf matches he had seen were at home on TV, and he was looking forward to seeing the players live, walking the course with them.

As he left the dining-room, he saw the tall, graceful woman of the preceding evening turn the far corner, approaching with a nonchalant long stride. She's better looking than I thought, he murmured to himself. She was dressed colourfully and expensively, in boots, tan skirt, a fawn sweater, a red scarf around her throat. Her black hair gleamed, cut in a short Dutch bob, framing her face.

Her smile barely contained mischievous merriment. "Good morning. I see you're out of your chair."

"I'm getting better at it," Stanwood said. "Just got off another one." He thumbed toward the dining-room.

"Wonderful. There's hope for us yet."

In the morning light, he couldn't decide if her eyes were tea-coloured. He asked the question before intending to. "Are you – uh – alone here?"

"I'm always alone. Tall girls are always alone. Unless they're on basketball teams, which I'm not. I'm Mary Garner."

Her smile was irresistible, making him smile, too. "Are you Irish, like the rest?" he asked.

"Not a bit. I'm from North Wales." Her eyes appraised him leisurely. "I know you're from the States, but can't guess – "

"Los Angeles. I'm Bill Stanwood." He felt hot, flushing. Ridiculous, he thought, but I've forgotten how to talk to women.

"I have some friends there," she said. "They're always after me to visit."

"You ought to take them up on it. It has its own good points."

"Perhaps I will. What sort of business are you in, Mr. Stanwood, if you don't mind my asking?"

He rubbed his wiry thick hair. "None, any more. I was a police detective of homicide. Retired last year after my wife died." Well, now she knows all about you, he thought, and that's the end of it.

The mocking merriment was gone from her eyes. "Oh, I'm so terribly sorry. I do go on being awfully nosy and now I've done it to you."

"It's all right. How about yourself? Ever been married?"

"Once," she said. "For a very short while. Although it seemed much longer, at the time."

"It's a matter of luck. You'll do better next time around."

"I certainly hope so." Her smile was back, warming him. "You seem to be on your way out. I don't suppose I can talk you into having coffee with me while I get some breakfast."

His regretful gesture made him feel clumsy. "I was on my way to the golf matches. I've never seen a real live one before. Maybe next time. I can't keep turning you down. You're too damn attractive."

"That's nice to hear. I was planning to be out there myself. Perhaps I'll see you out there in a while."

"Fine," he said. "I'll keep an eye out for you."

"No you won't," she said. "You'll let yourself become totally absorbed in the golfers and their game, and chase after them hole by hole, like all the others."

Stanwood rocked back on his heels, pleased by her gay directness, her bantering tone. "Well, I'll try not to be. But I'm curious about this tournament, apart from it being for charity. Do you know anything about it?"

"It's an annual event, nothing terribly important. Some pretty good players from Ireland, England, Scotland. A few of my own Welsh. The funds go to a local hospital for children."

"What about the danger of exposure?" he asked. "The odd bombing and sniping. Aren't they taking a big risk, all these big shots out in the open?"

She looked surprised. "I never thought of that. I suppose that's the police detective in you speaking."

"I guess so. They brought their security people along. That indicates they've considered the possibility, too."

She nodded soberly. "Nothing much ever happens in Rosslare. I've been coming here for years, seeing old friends, but really nothing like that has ever happened. There's always the first time, isn't there?"

"Sorry I mentioned it. I suppose I'm geared to see the worst in things. I'd better get out of here before I ruin your appetite for breakfast."

Her smile flashed immediately in response. "Oh, nothing can ever do that. Absolutely nothing. I wouldn't permit it."

"Good girl," Stanwood said, backing off. "Hope to see you later then."

She nodded, walking past him, and he was enveloped in the soft fragrance she was wearing. He watched her go in through the door to the dining-room, before he moved away.

That's a damn fine woman, he told himself. She wouldn't let you spoil things even though you were trying your best. Come along, you miserable soul. I'm taking you to a golf tournament. I want you to try and enjoy it.

Fourteen

Banners were strung in the air near the old clubhouse. ROSSLARE INTERNATIONAL 36-HOLES CHARITY ANNUAL. Ladies sat at small tables selling tickets. Stanwood paid his admission fee and received his ticket. As the woman pinned it on his jacket, he looked toward the first tee. There were no golfers there, no crowd of spectators. He was alone.

"Where's everybody?" he asked.

She waved her arm. "Out on the course, man. You'll be late the first few holes, for sure."

"Which way do I go?"

She handed him a scorecard bearing a design on the reverse of the course layout. "They'll be heading toward the sea the first few holes, then swing back inland the first nine." She put her finger on the diagram. "Here's about where the last group would be about now. The earlier ones just ahead. Good luck to you."

Stanwood paused. "These aren't professionals, are they?"

She rolled her eyes heavenward. "Saints, no! Amateurs all, but some are mighty fine golfers, as you'll be seeing."

As he walked down the first fairway, he saw a thin line of spectators at uneven intervals standing on small hilly vantage points. Others, partly hidden by bunkers and the cut of the high rough, were moving along the fairways in colourfully dressed clusters. The morning sun was bright, and Stanwood, feeling its warmth, experienced a strange tingling sensation of enjoyment as he headed toward the golf match just ahead. He felt young, like a boy entering the circus tent, awaiting all kinds of excitement and fun.

He was close enough to hear the tinny plunk of a ball as it fell into the cup. The player picked it up, the caddie restored the flag, and the group moved on. He quickened his step but saw immediately he would be too late to see them hit off the next tee. Other spectators, more knowledgeable of the game, were standing along the rough of the dogleg fairway to see the carry of the balls. Stanwood cut across the rough gorse in that direction, but before he could reach any vantage point heard the hard sound of the ball as it hit the ground. He looked toward the players on the tee, saw a moving blur, and again heard the sound of a ball hitting before he could watch its flight.

He looked ahead and saw other figures moving, strung out as far as he could see. Checking the diagram on the scorecard, he was able to chart a point where he could view two different holes, and if he missed one approaching, he would still be able to catch part of the beginning action for the next.

There was a double tee here. The fourth hole, a long dogleg curving north away from the sea, and the fourteenth, a short par-3, over a bunker just short of the water. The green was on a high knoll, and Stanwood hurried there. From this vantage point, he would be able to see the golfers' tee shots on both holes, and some of the play as they turned back after the first nine.

Behind the grassy knoll was an old shed, apparently a maintenance hut for the greenkeeper. A tractor behind. Below it, a narrow stretch of the beachfront.

He heard shouts of laughter, and saw a group of young children running around in a scrambling, tumbling game of tag. The disturbing antics of the Hallowe'en celebrants on the night before came to mind, and he smiled approvingly at kids playing the kind of harmless game he was used to.

He found his position to watch the golfers approaching. They would have to calculate the offshore wind, and draw their tee shots around the inland bend. It looked like the perfect place for him to see their skills.

The gallery was filtering outward to view the play, and Stanwood had an unobstructed line as the golfers teed up. The first man up seemed to swing too slowly. The ball soared high overhead and then began to turn with the wind. It came back in, took a big bounce, and scuttled perfectly down the fairway. The second man was less fortunate. His ball was sliced, curving too far to the right, with too much carry. It flew the fairway high over Stanwood's head, and fell close by into a huge bunker of thick, high grass.

Automatically, he hurried over to mark the ball before it was lost in the knee-high rough. There were peals of laughter behind him as the children came swarming up a path from the beach in pursuit of their runaway leader. Stanwood saw the boy duck into the maintenance shed from the corner of his eye. Walking carefully, he prodded about the grass and gorse, looking for the ball. He had marked its flight perfectly, and yet so thick was the ground cover, he couldn't find it.

The children were running all around him, and he held out his arms as if to block them from possibly trampling the ball. He raised his hand, waving to the approaching golfers to indicate the position, and fearful now of perhaps making matters worse for the errant golfer by his footprints, began to carefully climb out.

He heard shrill screams behind him. The youngsters were running out of the shed, white-faced and frightened. "Mister, mister," one shouted. "There's a dead one in there."

He ran up the steep grassy knoll, slipping midway, as the children stood outside the shed waiting. They were about to follow him inside, when he cautioned them off. "Better stay out here."

The shed interior was dark, relieved by light filtering through the uneven, worn planked sides. The dirt floor was hard, crowded with grass-cutting machinery, gardening tools, bags of fertilizer and seed. A power mower was angled in the corner toward the rear, and stepping around it Stanwood saw the still dark form sprawled stiffly on the ground. A heavy sigh escaped him.

Words chanted the previous evening sounded inside his head. "Death to the witch! Death to the witch!" His foot touched the black conical hat, and Stanwood, a veteran of homicide, stood shaken by the inert body clad in the black-booted grotesquerie of a witch's dress. So it hadn't been the innocent game after all, as he had feared, and now, in truth, this witch was dead.

The long cape had fallen over her head. He drew it back, and saw for the first time her hair, long and flaming red, damp and streaked darkly with blood. The mask had fallen off. He gently moved her hair away, and saw the battered, bludgeoned face. He bent and hunkered down, hearing the rasping of his breath.

"Well, Noreen," he crooned softly, "so there you are. And all the while, I thought you were trying to avoid me."

The body was cold and damp, its frailty stiffening with the cold and approaching rigor of death. He looked absently around for the bludgeoning murder weapon, hearing in his mind words he knew by rote from countless medical examiners, for his homicide reports. "Death due to subdural haematoma resulting from blunt force trauma of the head."

The shed was littered with gardening tools and machinery. Any of the metal objects could have done the deed. He heard tittering breathless sounds. The children were looking in the open doorway, their faces streaked with dirt, their eyes huge with dread and curiosity.

"Yes, she's dead," he said softly. "But you'll have to stay outside there." They remained, drawn by the drama, and he added, "The police will have to check the floor and everything for prints. Do you understand?"

"Who is it?" a small girl asked. "Do we know her?"

"I can't say," he said. "You'll find out soon enough." He stood up slowly and walked toward the door. They retreated in awe of his towering presence, and as he stepped outside, he heard himself asking what was a very strange question for him.

"I wonder if one of you would mind finding a policeman."

They broke away then, running off to scream about the dead lady in the shed. Stanwood stood rooted in the open doorway as spectators, oblivious now to the golfers, ran toward him.

The crowd jammed around him as he stood blocking their entrance to the shed. He remained silent, merely shaking his head to their questions. They waited sullenly, curious, but nobody dared challenge him.

He saw the golfers on the green looking on, their play interrupted. One of the security men was making his way up to the knoll. "What's the trouble, mate?"

he asked.

Stanwood wondered how to answer him. Finally he said, "The kids were playing around. Found a body inside. A girl's been murdered."

The man's lip twitched. "And what are you doing here?"

"The same as you," Stanwood said. "Waiting for the police."

Fifteen

The local peace officer was Albert Rattigan. They were called garda in Ireland, he explained, not policemen. "I've put a call in to Wexford," he said. "They'll be sending their experts over. Task force and somebody to identify the deceased."

"Her name is Noreen Kelly," Stanwood said.

Rattigan leaned back. "Begging your pardon, sir, but you not being from these parts, how do you know that?"

"She's my sister-in-law." The constable looked sceptical and Stanwood opened his billfold. The bronze insignia and ID card was a small part of his past he held on to.

"Lieutenant of the Los Angeles Police Department, Detective Bureau of Homicide." Rattigan was reading it off, sounding impressed. "What, may I ask then, brings you to Rosslare in Ireland?"

"My wife died. I came to see *her*."

The constable sighed, genuinely touched. "Ah, a pity it is, sir. You have my sympathy."

Stanwood nodded silently. Mary Garner was making her way through the crowd. Still stricken, he looked at her without recognition, unsmiling. She came up breathing hard. "I heard."

Stanwood looked at her without warmth. "Heard what?"

She was startled. "Why, that somebody's been murdered."

Stanwood nodded. Then he found himself telling her what he had just told the local officer. He heard himself, as if from a great distance, speaking without emotion, in his usual official voice.

In shocked reflex, she bit her lower lip. Stanwood saw, and chided himself. You see the moist red lip, all right, the white teeth, the sympathy she's giving you, her tenderness. And yet, for all the time you spent inside there with Katie's own Noreen, you didn't see a thing. Nothing but her body, not one single bloody clue. No doubt at all about your being a retired detective.

He heard a wailing siren and saw a small van driving up the fairway. "That'll be the gardai from Wexford," the local man said. "That's where they'll be taking the body. After the doctor does his findings, sir."

The woman touched his sleeve. "My car's in the parking lot, Bill. I'll drive you there."

"Thanks," he said. "It'll give me a chance to have my cry."

PART TWO
Sixteen

The two Irish detectives sat across a table from him in the police station of Wexford on Old Jail Road. "This is Detective Goggin. I'm Detective Shaw," the wiry, sad-faced man said. "Constable's report states that you are a former police officer yourself. Would you elaborate?"

Stanwood felt strange on the opposite side of an interrogation team. "I've retired officially from the force. I was lieutenant, commander of a detective division in West Los Angeles for ten years." He sat back appraising them and their methods.

"Number of men under your command?"

"Thirty, on average. We covered an area of twenty square miles."

Shaw was asking the questions, Goggin taking notes. " 'Homicide', the report said."

Stanwood, nodding, placed his open billfold on the table for them. "They kept us busy. How's it with you fellows?"

Shaw appeared not to have heard. He was studying the ID card, examining Stanwood's photo and comparing. He tossed the billfold to the other

61

detective. "Reason for retirement?"

"Personal."

He's a stiff one, Goggin thought. Steely-eyed bastard. I wouldn't want to be working under him. He'd have me at it full time. I know the type. The bugger who won't quit.

Shaw was waving his hand, not yet ready to share his partner's vision. "Please, Mr. Stanwood. We know of your relationship with the Kelly girl. You're one of us, if a stranger, and we want to do all we can to help."

That says it, Johnny boy, thought Goggin. But don't go overboard with it. We've got a big enough case load, as is. The Yank's a bigshot detective. Let him figure it out.

Shaw said, "Would you be so good as to explain retirement at your age? You could have done another twenty years."

"No way," Stanwood said. "After my wife Katie died, there didn't seem to be any reason for anything. Working, living – " He wagged his head forcefully. What the hell am I telling them the story of my life for? They've got their own problems. "I decided I wasn't mentally equipped for the job any longer. Too much for me to handle. So I quit."

"Too bad," Shaw said. "Maybe a breather, a change, would have been all you needed."

"Who knows? It's over and done with. Why waste time? I'd like to find out something about Noreen. Who she knew, how did a thing like this happen? She was my wife's kid sister, but otherwise a stranger to me."

"We'll be going into that. You know how an investigation works. It takes time. Rest assured Detective Goggin and I will do all we possibly can."

It struck Stanwood then how many countless times he had made the same glib statement to friends or relatives of the victim. "I saw her one time, at noon, the day I came in. This past Thursday. Briefly, later, I got a phone message from her, at the hotel, or presumably from her, to meet me at a tavern here in Wexford. Cullimore's."

"You qualified that," Shaw said. "*Presumably* from her?"

"A new girl at the switchboard didn't know Noreen's voice. I assumed it was from her. I don't know anybody else here."

"What time were you to meet?"

"The message said at four. I waited until five-thirty."

"And that was the last time you saw her – Thursday."

Stanwood nodded. "Unless you count last night. Kids were running through the hotel grounds. Caught a witch, they said. And they had one looped and tied in the middle. Whipping her lightly with a long rod.

"They were chanting this odd tune. 'Death to the witch! Death to the witch!' Beating her on the cadence end of it. I didn't like the look of it. People around me were smiling. Fellow next to me implied it was a local custom at All Hallows."

Shaw shook his head. "Not to my knowledge. And I'm born here and been around all its parts. The idea of a witch, yes. Capturing and beating a live one, no. Absolutely. My word on that." He turned to the husky man beside him. "You ever, Goggin?" The man shook his head, emphatically negative. "If it was me there, I'd have murdered the little bastards."

"It bothered me," Stanwood said, "but I figured I was wrong. I should have known better when I stood up."

"What was that, sir?" Shaw said.

"It seemed to me the witch then tried to escape – break out of the group. Perhaps she saw me – if it was Noreen. Anyway, they dragged her back, and marched her off. They went out of sight, her still caught in the middle, the kids chanting that same ugly tune."

"You heard nothing from her – no sign of recognition – no cry for help?"

"Well, I took that abortive break she made as a sign." He was thinking grimly. "Then when they were out of sight, going down the road in front of the hotel, I thought I heard somebody cry out. It didn't sound human, then. A wailing, awful sound. I suppose I didn't want to think it was human, the witch crying out, and I dismissed it from my mind."

"This all happened about what time?"

"About nine – nine thirty. You'll have half the hotel who were sitting out there with me as witnesses."

"The costume she was wearing when you discovered the body – the same as the witch caught up in the mob?"

Stanwood thought silently a long moment, then shrugged again. "It seemed the same. A witch's costume. The cape, the mask, the long pointed brimmed hat. We've all seen it often enough. I'm not convinced the kids killed her. Not at all. But I'd say Noreen was the witch they had." Goggin was writing fast. "My guess is she was afraid of something, was on the run. Couldn't make it at Cullimore's. Tried to disguise herself as a witch, at Hallowe'en. The kids must have caught her in Rosslare and made her part of their game."

"We'll check all of that," Shaw said softly.

"Well, that's another thing," Stanwood said, spreading his hands. "I'd like to get in on this with you, if I can."

He noticed Goggin closing his little book a split second before Shaw stood up. They knew their own ways, these two. "I'm sorry, Mr. Stanwood," Shaw said. "According to Irish law, there is no possible way you can interfere, or help, as you might wish to call it. Even if you were still employed as a Detective Commander of your division of detectives, you would be out of your jurisdiction, and in penalty of the law if you attempted to assist in our investigation."

Bullshit, Goggin thought. Let him try it and fall on his ass.

"I figured you to say that. What if I conduct my own?"

Shaw was buttoning his topcoat. "If you like, I can take the matter up with our Chief Superintendent in Dublin in charge of Criminal Investigation."

Stanwood stood up, too. "Don't bother. I know what he will say, too."

As they were shaking hands, Shaw said, "You're staying at the Strand Hotel in Rosslare? Can Detective Goggin and I drop you off there?"

Stanwood shook his head. "No, thanks. I have my own ride waiting in the next room. Unless she's taken off and gone back without me."

He was relieved, nevertheless, when they stepped out into the waiting room, to see her still there, sitting erect and utterly composed, as if she had sat in police stations before for hours while the gentleman she had been with was being questioned.

Seventeen

She handled her small expensive car with easy assurance, her gloved hands deftly manoeuvring the wheel through the narrow crowded streets. The town of Wexford seemed to be always on holiday, he thought. The tourists had found it out and were swarming purposefully through it.

"Those two detectives you were with," she said, "are they assigned to the investigation?"

"Yes. The tall one is Detective Shaw. The shorter, husky man is Goggin, similar rank. They seem capable."

"I would imagine it had to be a strange experience for you. I mean, being on the other side of an interrogation."

He looked at her. "You're very perceptive. It was. They could have asked a lot more. No doubt we'll be seeing more of each other."

"Why is that?"

"I gave something away and they didn't pick me up on it. I said Noreen was on the run. That she couldn't keep our date at the tavern, and tried disguising herself as a witch at Hallowe'en."

"You're the detective," she said, "but I don't see that they go together. She might not have been able to keep the appointment for different reasons. And, as for the witch's costume, she might have worn it to a party, for all you know."

"Possible," Stanwood said. "All we need to confirm that would be volunteer witnesses from the alleged party. I don't know who she knows here, nothing about her personal life."

"I suppose you're assuming, too, that she was the witch caught up by the kids last night, too."

Stanwood flexed his hands. "You saw that, too?"

"I was still out there on the terrace. Farther up the incline of the miniature golf layout. Certainly I saw it."

"What did you think of it?"

"I thought it was awful. What else could one think? It seemed very odd to me that nobody there, none of the hotel guests, tried to get her away, or help in any way."

"I wanted to, but the gentleman on my right was laughing himself sick over it. Assured me it goes on every year here. Local game custom on All-Hallows Eve."

"That's utter nonsense. It was cruel. But then I happen to know rather well how cruel children can be."

"How's that?" he asked.

"I have a small school for handicapped children in Wales. All of them have been bullied, tormented one way or another in their lives because of their disorders or infirmities."

"Good for you. I'd have thought from your looks and voice you were an actress. Stage or TV."

She laughed. "Well, I was, for a time. But you have to turn yourself into too many people. I'd much rather be myself."

"Makes sense. I had the feeling you were something special, or at least did something special."

She laughed. "Make up your mind. Which is it?"

"Give me time. You'll be the very next mystery I work on, I promise."

"It can wait," she said. "I don't suppose any of the kids running around the hotel last night with their captive will volunteer any information. Now that she's dead."

"Before you were saying it didn't necessarily have to be the same witch."

"Yes, but the children don't know that, do they?" She stopped as a huge lorry filling the entire street turned the corner, blocking it. "They'll have to assume it's their witch, won't they? They'd be afraid to admit anything now."

Stanwood shrugged. "Rattigan, the local officer, might nose it out. And then Shaw and Goggin might get to the bottom of it fast. Don't forget my wife and her sister both came from Rosslare. Their mother, I understand, still lives there."

"You'll be seeing her soon, I imagine, won't you?"

"Right after I find the boy with the light hair who drives a little yellow car."

She glanced sideways at him. "What does that mean?"

"The first and only time I saw Noreen. She was still alive when she stepped into his car."

"Did you mention that to the detectives back there?"

"As a matter of fact," Stanwood said slowly, "I didn't."

"That's understandable," she said. "You forgot, I suppose."

Stanwood was shaking his head. "No, I didn't forget."

"Well, I suppose you know what you're doing. At heart, I guess, you're still a detective of homicide."

Stanwood was gazing out of the window, his eyes closely following each passerby before shifting to the next. "That's what I aim to find out. If I still am."

"And I suppose," she said lightly, "when you find the killer, you'll have your own vengeance, destroy him with your own hands."

Stanwood shook his head negative again. "No, I don't work that way. Never did. Don't be deceived by my size and looks. I've never permitted my emotions to enter into it. It's up to the courts to decide punishment, not me."

He happened to look at his hands, still curling and flexing, and wondered if it was all over for him at last, that his words were a lie now, and he would never again be a rational human being.

Her black gloved hands were trying to get a cigarette from a pack on the seat, while steering. "Damn," she said.

"What's wrong?"

She lifted her left hand. A hole at the tip had snagged her left forefinger. "I've been meaning to buy a new pair. But these are so comfortable, I can't seem to give them up."

He got the cigarette loose for her, placed it between her lips, and lit it with her lighter. She thanked him and he nodded absently. With all her class, she's like me, a sentimental slob; hates to give things up.

Eighteen

Goggin was behind the wheel when Detective Shaw folded his lank body in beside him. "What do you think of him?" Shaw said.

"The Yank? Bloody tough man, that."

Shaw nodded imperceptibly, lighting his pipe. "Knows this game, wouldn't you say?"

"Aye. He's got the hard look of experience, John."

"You know," Shaw said, "that city he's from. Los Angeles. I happened to be studying their crime rate recently. They lead his country in homicides."

"Too much money there, for a fact. But for a poor country, we're not doing too badly at it ourselves. And did you read the paper just in about the other side getting the woman and her husband up in County Tyrone, outside Belfast?"

"Aye, I did, but she's been asking for the trouble right along, hasn't she now? What about this one we got here?"

Goggin shrugged thick bulky shoulders. His clothing always seemed to draw in on him, becoming tighter and tighter. "The Kelly girl? I was expecting something different, you know, along with them golfers coming down here for their game."

"There's still that chance," Shaw said. "They play another round tomorrow. I don't figure how Noreen Kelly from Rosslare enters into that, do you?"

"If we knew, why would we be sitting here talking?"

"You think the Yank is going to sit back and wait for us to solve this one for him?"

Goggin uttered a short derisive snort. "Not bloody likely."

"The man up in Dublin Castle, he won't like it one little bit, Michael, if some bloody old Yank comes up with the murderer before we do."

Goggin nodded. "No, he won't like it, not at all, he won't. Have you spoken to him yet on this?"

"Not directly to the Chief Superintendent, I didn't. But I did just call the office there. Inspector Moore will be running a check on William Stanwood for us. Then we'll know if he's all he seems."

"Aye. And what will we be doing in the meanwhile?"

"I've put the men out to look for the murder weapon. That might give us something to go on. And we'll be running a check on Noreen Kelly, sending her prints around to Dublin and Belfast."

Goggin's thick hands curled over the steering wheel. "Aye, but what now, John?"

"Get this bloody car going," Shaw said. "We have to move fast on this one." As Goggin looked at him with questioning eyes, he added, "Don't ask me where, man. It'll come to me."

Nineteen

They passed McSwiney's Pub. Stanwood remembered it as a favourite watering-place of the cabbie, Paddy Moran. "If you can find a place somewhere around here to park," he said, "I'd like to stop in there."

"There are better places, you know."

"No doubt. But a cabbie I know likes it. If he comes along, I'll need him to get me around. Meanwhile, we can have ourselves a drink."

"All right, Bill. But I'd like you to know I'm at your disposal if you want me to take you anywhere. Or you can have my car any time you wish."

"Thanks, but I'd rather use Moran. You never know what you'll be running into in these matters, and I'd rather you're not involved. As for borrowing your car, it's more or less the same thing. Paddy Moran knows the area, and can save me time blundering about."

She found parking space for the little MG near the corner. Street traffic was heavy as they walked back. "Is it always like this?" he asked.

"It's about average. Wexford town is a genuine tourist attraction. It has a long history, and all the quaintness you would want for your shopping experience or camera."

"We have some back alleys where I come from that are wider than some of these streets."

They had to separate and walk single file for a few yards as energetic throngs swarmed on relentlessly. "Still, it doesn't bother the tourists. In fact, I think they rather enjoy the experience."

Moran's old Rover was nowhere to be seen. McSwiney's was smaller than Cullimore's, but comfortable like any old pub. Stanwood walked directly to the bartender.

"Has Paddy Moran been in yet today?"

"Not yet, he ain't. But if you'll be having a table with the lady, he might still be in before you finish your drink."

"Are you Mr. McSwiney?"

"Aye, that I am."

He took the order for their drinks, and brought them over. The table surface was clean, but he swabbed it thoroughly with his rag. "Don't mind the looks of the place, miss. It ain't elegant, but it's clean, and me missus does a meat pie fit for the Berkeley Court in Dublin itself."

The wide smile that had attracted Stanwood reappeared on her face. "You wouldn't happen to have one handy, just to prove it?" she said.

As if suddenly aware it was too soon to be gay, she looked apologetically at Stanwood. "It's okay," he said. "Make it two, then, and I'll find out, as well."

McSwiney departed for the rear kitchen and Stanwood lifted his glass. "I don't want you tiptoeing around me," he said. "It was the same when I had Katie. It's my own problem and I don't put it on anybody."

"I don't understand how you go about this. I've read mystery novels, and they're solved usually to my satisfaction. The real live cases in the newspapers are something else. A crime is committed, there seems to be nothing linking killer with victim, and yet in a few months or so, I read the police have come up with him."

"As a rule, yes, but not always. Some get away."

"Is it all right to talk about this – this – ?"

"Absolutely. It might even help, talking about it."

"All right, then. You told me you know very little about Noreen Kelly. Nothing about her personal life, at all. You don't have the murder weapon. No idea of the killer. How do you start? It all seems quite impossible to me."

"No, not impossible," Stanwood said slowly. "It's difficult putting the pieces together. Because a puzzle is what it is, nearly always. Who would want to do this thing, and why?"

"But you know nothing of her background," she protested. "Where are the links? How do you weed out the possibilities?"

"There's usually no divine inspiration. You do it one thing at a time. You add up and you eliminate. You start with nothing, and go on from there."

"It doesn't sound very promising."

He stared at her. She was a very lovely woman, he thought. Warm and intelligent, with quick wit and composure. A good one to be around. Yet he wanted her out of the way so he could get going on this, not have to give civilized answers to her reasonable questions. "No, it's not too promising." Noreen's odd response of unreasoning fear that first day came into his mind. He didn't want to talk about that, either, any more than he had with the detectives a while back. He shifted uncomfortably in his chair, knowing there would come a point where he would have to cut her off, perhaps hurt her feelings.

The owner-bartender returned bearing his own treasures, giving Stanwood the respite he needed. "Here you are, then. Soon you'll be telling the world about Molly McSwiney's own pie."

She lifted her fork cheerfully. "Well, Mr. McSwiney, I do like a devoted husband, whatever the risk."

She's left-handed, Stanwood thought, remembering at once the one-sided attack on Noreen Kelly's face, done with a brutal left-handed blow. Strong hands, too. He caught himself up, shaking his head. Oh, William, will you ever stop it? Get on with the pie, man. Obedient to his thought, he dipped in.

He smiled at the waiting owner. "Delicious, Mr. McSwiney. My compliments to the chef."

"Make that unanimous, Mr. McSwiney, I don't suppose you're giving out the secret recipe?"

McSwiney looked unhappy. "Well, miss, now if I was to do that, sure and it wouldn't be a secret no more, now would it?" He backed off, and then turned calling to the door. "Come over here, man, and I'll be bringing you your glass. This gentleman is here asking for the likes of you."

Moran, blinking to adjust to the light, stopped halfway to the bar and came shuffling over slowly. At sight of Stanwood, he stopped, drawing himself up. "Is it you, then, having a hearty meal after the news I've been hearing? Sure and your heart must be breaking, man."

Stanwood nodded. "It's not the first time, Paddy. Pull up a chair. We've got some business to discuss."

The cabbie hesitated over his chair, peering intently across the table at the woman. "Aye," he said, "and that's a fair enough colleen you've found yourself. You'll be introducing me, no doubt, before the business we're to be discussing."

Stanwood laughed. Maybe it's the Irish in him, he thought, but he works like a charm with me. "Mary Garner," he said, "meet Paddy Moran."

"Pleased to meet you, Mr. Moran," she said smiling.

"Aye, and I'm thinking I've had the pleasure before."

Stanwood saw her smile fade and quickly return. "I don't think so," she said, and Stanwood watching, told himself, she's lying. He caught himself up at once. Save it for what you have to do. It's her own life and business, and I've got mine.

Twenty

The lane to Cedar View Burrow in Rosslare was unpaved, wheel-rutted and pocked with small sharp stones. The old Rover sedan took it slowly with care. "A few more like this one," Paddy Moran said over his shoulder, "and you'll be after buying me a set of new tyres."

"Listen," Stanwood said, "before we're done here, with what I'm paying, you'll be able to afford a new car."

"Could be. But it won't last near as good as this one." Moran patted his wheel affectionately. "I'm thinking I'd sooner give up me missus than this old boy."

Stanwood heard the cabbie's grumbled concern with easy tolerance. Since parting from Mary Garner a short while back, and hiring Paddy Moran again, he had felt strangely calm. The grief had been replaced by a familiar drive to bring a murderer to account. It seemed like old times.

It was near dusk, the late afternoon sun filtering through a solitary stand of cedars. They were in the outer limits of Rosslare, across the main street. Moran had found the nondescript lane with little difficulty, although as he claimed, the old Rover did it for him. "It smells out the streets, and that's a fact. I've no idea of how it works. Never been here before."

The area was flat, grazing pastures and farm land. The houses were few and widely separated. Caravans tenanted vacant lots, wash hanging from lines along the clustered trailers.

"Who lives in those things?" Stanwood asked.

"The caravans? Some are drifters, others long-term tenants. The rent is not high, and they have the light and water. Some been living there for years, bringing up their kids, sending them off to school like normal folks. It ain't fancy, mind, but where else can one live cheap these days?"

Stanwood nodded absently, his mind snapping back to his immediate purpose. "Matt Bogson," he said. "Noreen Kelly's stepfather. Know anything about him, Paddy?"

"Not the smallest bit. Maybe if I'd seen the man in a bar or pub first, then maybe I'd know him. Wexford town's where I hang me cap, and never have I heard his name there."

"Three years," Stanwood said as if to himself. "The girl at the hotel said he'd been with Mrs. Kelly that long. Noreen left home for good about that time, judging from the last letter we got."

"It don't mean the man drove her off," Moran said. "Lots of girls leave the nest after the old man dies. A good thing for some, too. What've they got here?"

It was a question Kate had asked herself, he realized, and left without looking back. Now as he approached the house, he wondered how it would go. His original intention had been to talk of Kate with her mother. Noreen was alive then. It was a disheartening prospect. He pictured the old lady frail and broken.

The Kelly house was old, ugly and small. The exterior was darkened red stone with paint-flecked wood trim. The garden was a patch of withered plants and the grass needed trimming. There was a garage and work shed at the side, a pickup truck in front.

He assumed the police had already been here, or neighbours who had heard the news. He got out of the Rover, left Moran to wait, and knocked at the door.

Heavy footsteps sounded inside. The door opened and a large, shaggy-haired man stood there, a hostile glint in his small, muddy yellow eyes. "Yas, what is it?"

"Mr. Bogson?"

"Aye? You another copper?"

"No, my name is Stanwood. I was married to Kate Kelly. Her mother would know my name. Is she in?"

"Aye, she'll be in the back room. Might be, she'll talk with ye."

Bogson was older, thick-shouldered, bigger and heavier than Stanwood. As he followed the broad back, Stanwood was thinking, stronger, too, even at his age. Got hands like shovels. Not a friendly soul, is he? Speaks like a farmer, but he's shrewd. Don't like that look in his eyes. Dangerous man to be about. Noreen was smart getting out.

Bogson led the way through small dark rooms, his tread heavy on the hardwood flooring. At the far end, he stopped and leaned his massive head through the open doorway.

"You'll have coompany," he announced. "The mon says he was married to yer eldest. Will ye be wanting to see him?" There was the soft sound of an answering voice, almost inaudible. He turned to Stanwood. "All right, then. In ye go, and don't weary the poor woman about it all."

Stanwood didn't move. "I'd rather you come in with me. I want you to hear what I have to say, and I'd like to ask you some questions, too, while I'm here."

Matt Bogson's eyes glared angrily at him. "No need for me. It's not my lot."

"I agree, but I'd appreciate it if you'd stay. I'm not a copper, not any more. But I was one, the better part of my life. A detective, where I come from. And while I'm here, I'd like to see what I can do to clear up Noreen's murder."

Bogson eyed him stubbornly. "The lass is dead. What good can coom of it now? You don't know the sort she was, no more than I, and I knew her some. You'll be spending the rest of yer days here if yer trying to work out the reasons."

"Let him come in, Matt. No use bullying the man. He was married to my daughter, now be civilized."

The voice, although soft, carried its own steely thrust, and Stanwood was surprised to see its effect on the giant at his side.

"All right, love," he said quietly. "Come along, then."

The room was brighter, with soft cushioned chairs, dainty feminine furnishings. A fireplace glowed with red coals showing through the ash. There were pictures on the walls, landscapes, seascapes, and paintings of flowers. There was no doubt about this being her room.

She sat in a low stuffed flowered chair, a rug over her knees, her shoulders draped by a thick woollen shawl. She seemed frail, sitting without movement, and the only sign of life was in her eyes. Brilliant blue like Kate's, and Noreen's, too, he remembered. He looked for a cane or wheelchair nearby and saw neither, leaving him to wonder if she were crippled or paralyzed by a stroke. The warmth of the fire apparently had no effect upon her bundled body.

Her voice was sharp, with an energetic bite to it. "Well, then, Mr. Stanwood, am I seeing you at last in my own house?"

He nodded, standing quietly before her. Now what am I going to talk about first, he wondered, Kate or Noreen? His own voice, when he found it, sounded the same as always to him.

"Kate wrote you often," he said. And you never replied, he wanted to add. Were you begrudging her a new life? "We were planning to visit you, but then she became ill. It went too fast, and soon any trip at all was out of the question." She sat there, the beautiful eyes untroubled, unblinking. "She wrote you about it," he said, trying to keep the hardness out of his tone.

"There was no need to write," she said. "Kate knew I loved her."

There was another chair near her, and he decided to take it, unbidden, to counter the rage rising inside him. Bogson stood against the far wall quietly, his yellow eyes watchful. "I think she would have liked hearing from you," Stanwood said. "She wrote her father, too. Mr. Kelly never answered, either."

"Yes, I know all that," she said. "This is my house, you'll remember."

Beautiful, he thought. What the hell am I doing here anyway? There's a lot of hate in this house, and I can see now why Kate left early. "In any event," he said evenly, "when Kate was dying, we decided it would be a nice idea for me to come out here. She wanted Noreen to have some of her things. Some pictures, taken when she was younger and healthy. Her ring. A few personal mementoes. After she died, I quit my job. I had an address for Noreen up in Dublin but she'd moved on. Then a girl at a hotel there told me she might have come back to Rosslare. I met her by accident my first day at the hotel. She was running out, promised to get in touch with me. She called once but couldn't keep our date. I didn't see her again until this morning, when I found her body on the golf course."

Bogson moved his feet. "Yas, we know about that. The gardai they already been here."

Neither of them appeared moved by grief, seemingly untouched by the brutal incident. Stanwood was beginning to doubt his senses. "You know how she was murdered, of course," he said.

Bogson nodded. "Yas, they told us that."

"Struck with something, they said. Over the head, was it?" the woman said.

"I don't suppose either of you know who might have done this?" Stanwood said.

"Nowt," Bogson said. "How would we be knowing the murderer?"

"She was always here and there," Mrs. Kelly said. "It might be anybody, now, might it not?"

Stay in there, Stanwood told himself. Don't let them put you off. "Well, perhaps you can tell me, Mrs. Kelly – or is it Mrs. Bogson now –" He waited, and drew no response. "Perhaps you are familiar with some of her boy friends. A name or two, people I could talk to."

"Nowt," Bogson said curtly. "She be not here that much, mon. When I coom to this house, she left for good. Not a word to me or her mother sitting here. Just off with herself and what things she had left in her drawer."

"When was that?"

"Past three year ago. Right, love?"

"Just past," she said.

"Well, perhaps the name of a girl friend she had?"

The woman's voice sounded more strident. "I'll not be knowing. Never did she bring anybody here to her home. Ashamed of us, she was. Like her sister before her. And just as wild. There's no telling."

Stanwood swallowed the rising gorge in his throat. "You're telling me, ma'am, you know nothing of your daughter's life? She was brought up here, went to school. She must have had friends."

"Well, then, you might ask them about it. And if her dead father was here, he'd be telling you the same."

Stanwood looked at Bogson. "Perhaps Mrs. Kelly is limited because of her confinement to the chair. You get around. Are you telling me the same? You know nothing of her friends, what sort she went with?"

Bogson stepped away from the wall. Stanwood was getting to his feet, seeing the dogged look of the man. Bogson stopped abruptly, his big hands trembling. "Look, mon. There's nowt to say. She was here and there. To Belfast, Dublin and back. She did things that was wild, and always coming home scared. I niver asked her what, nor did she say. Now the lass is dead. Is nowt more to talk over. Am I saying it right, love?"

"Thank you for calling, Mr. Stanwood. You'll not be staying long in Rosslare?"

Stanwood shook his head. "I never said that, Mrs. Kelly. If I find out anything, I'll take it to the police."

Bogson walked him to the door and threw it open. Dusk was settling, the sky purple with grey-streaked clouds. As Stanwood passed him, he said, "Don't mind the look of the house, mon. I'm rich and can give her the best. I'm in the construction business. But she won't move out. Says this is her house to stay, for living and dying."

"How rich are you?" Stanwood asked, bemused.

The old man shrugged. Then he lifted his thick arm, swinging it toward the sea and horizon. "I own all the caravans out there, all the land. It hurts me not to be giving her the best. But you see how she is. And here I can be buying her the richest house in all Rosslare."

"Does she give you a reason, Mr. Bogson?"

"Nowt."

"Do you happen to know why she hates her daughters?"

Bogson stared at him. "It's not hate, mon. The woman's not the one to show love, is all."

"She doesn't appear to be able to move. Do you have any idea of what's wrong with her?"

Bogson looked at the sky solemnly. "God's will, she says."

"Amen to that," Stanwood said. The door closed behind him. As he approached the Rover, in the murky twilight, the headlights came on.

"Did it go all right?" Moran asked.

"Not bad," Stanwood said. "I didn't kill either one of them."

Twenty-One

It was dark when Moran dropped him off at the Strand. Stanwood got out slowly. "Tomorrow's Sunday, and I'll be taking in the second part of the golf match. I don't expect you to be giving up your day off, Paddy. Make it as early as you can Monday morning, and we'll cruise some more. Okay?"

"Fine, sir. And if you don't mind my saying, sir, don't take it so to heart. I can see it in your face what went on back there. As someone put it, tomorrow's another day."

Stanwood nodded. "Could be. Maybe the girl's murder was just a smokescreen for the real happening. If that ties up, one of those golfing VIPs might be catching a bullet."

"Well, I'll be home with the missus if you'd be wanting me. You have me card with the number. And if there's a thing or two you want done, say it now and I'll try to do it."

"Listen, anything will do. I came here not knowing a thing, and now I know even less. I've got to find out something about Noreen's personal life. Anybody she knew or went with. Do you think your friend McSwiney knows Tim Cullimore?"

"I'll be dropping in for my pint on the way home, sir. I'll put it to him then. I remember now you were saying Tim knew more about the girl than he let go."

"Well, let's say he was cautious, and I respect him for that. But it's a different matter now she's dead. He might want to help me."

"You'll not be forgetting, sir, the detectives from Wexford might be on to him, too, sir, and asking the same."

"Sure, well, this isn't a contest, exactly. They're within their rights telling me to stay out of it. If it wasn't a family affair now, I'd let them have it all."

"Right, sir. But maybe you have another one to be asking around about, just in case they already have Tim to the ground."

"The last time I saw Noreen, she was stepping into a small yellow car. Kid with light hair was at the wheel. If you can come up with that one, Paddy, I'll double the rate."

Moran held up his hand. "Now no need for that, sir. You can't do no better for me than you already been. Would you know the make of car? Fiat, maybe Japanese or the German bug?"

"It was raining hard. I couldn't make it out. I'm pretty sure it wasn't the VW, but I'm not too familiar with all the small car models here. If it wasn't a Fiat, it was some other small sedan. I'll try to study what's around meanwhile." He slammed a big fist into his hand. "Those bastards at the house gave me nothing, not a damn thing. Noreen was an attractive girl. There should have been dozens after her, and some she liked. No way that girl was invisible."

"You don't happen to have a picture of her now, do you, sir?"

Stanwood grunted. "The last one was taken when she was very young. No resemblance now. Why?"

"I was thinking if you had one, you might be taking it around to the dances."

"Dances?"

"Oh, aye. That's where most the young girls go to around these parts. With their lads, or to meet others there."

"What kind of dance places? Where do I look?"

"There's the Shamrock, over to Waterford. There's the Wexford Bull and Art Course nearer to where I live."

Stanwood was nodding, when suddenly he reached into his pocket. "Dammit, what the hell's wrong with me? Of course, I have a picture. Here's what she looked like."

Moran looked over the small, coloured photo. "That's a real pretty colleen, sir. And is that a recent picture of her?"

Stanwood shook his head and retrieved the photo. "No, as a matter of fact, Paddy, that's a picture of my wife Kate." He saw the puzzled stare on the cabbie's face. "It struck me when we met in the hotel lobby first day. Noreen is the dead spitting image of Katie. Same eyes, same colour hair, same heart-shaped face. Same – "

Moran put his car into gear. "It's all right, sir, and I'll be saying good night, and seeing you soon."

Twenty-Two

High up in Dublin Castle, the sprawling fortress-like administrative complex near the centre of the Irish capital, Chief Superintendent Marlon Gallagher sat in his Detective Branch office. He was a large, imposing man who had worked his way up the ranks without benefit of college degrees, or knowing the right people. And although his Crime Section offices had the most modern laboratory equipment and highly skilled technicians, he never passed over the fundamentals of solid, persevering, foot-slogging detective work.

Another man was with him now, his deputy, Detective Inspector Amos Moore, smaller, more intensive looking. He placed a sheet of paper on the super's desk. "Report of a murder in Rosslare. Local girl but been away from home. Name of Noreen Kelly. Detectives Shaw and Goggin are in charge from Wexford."

"Rosslare? Isn't that where they're having the golf match this weekend?"

"That's the point of the report, sir. Her body was discovered on the golf course."

Gallagher's heavy eyebrows arched. "Think there's any connection, Amos, politically? We've put our security people out there to guard the visiting golfers."

"Nothing on that aspect, sir. On the surface, it seems to be the result of some All-Hallows Eve pranksters laying it on too thick."

"Well, keep me informed."

Moore persisted. "You'd better read it, sir. There's another element added. A detective just recently retired from the Los Angeles police is visiting Rosslare. William Stanwood. The victim is his wife's younger sister. Stanwood's wife Kate Kelly died last year and he seems inclined to get into this."

The super read the report and chuckled. "As I understand this, it's the complication of some international competition in finding the murderer."

"Detective Shaw's feeling is the copper from Los Angeles won't stay out of it. He's hinting at instructions, sir."

Gallagher studied the report again. "Commander of Detective Bureau Homicide Los Angeles county. Do you know, Amos, they led the entire United States in homicides last year? Over two thousand, I'm told. Must be more to the place than TV and flicks."

"That's probably what's got Shaw and Goggin stirred up. The man's record is of the finest. I've just run a check on Lieutenant Stanwood. He's got a lot of experience going for him."

"Interesting," Gallagher said.

Moore looked closely at his superior, trying to penetrate the unflappable mask. "Still and all," he said cautiously, "he'll be working it out on his own. No help from us."

Gallagher was thinking, What a wonderful opportunity for a man to see what he can do. Smiling broadly, he said, "It's a classic confrontation, you know. Shaw and Goggin, and whoever else they call in, will be working with the lab boys, the expert forensic people, the criminalist technicians with their white coats, and ultraviolet machines, and microscopes that can identify a splinter of glass, a mite of dust, or a single strand of hair. The print people and pathologists. The American will be on his own, as you say. Nothing to help him but his own instincts. Putting the pieces of the puzzle together the old way."

"Well, sir, he does have one advantage."

"Tell me, then."

"His rage, sir. Doing in his wife's kid sister."

The super nodded, gazing far out the window. "If they want him out of it, I won't have it, Amos. Understand? I want the Yank to have his own run at it."

"I'll make a note to the effect. Any particular reason, sir? You'll be going against your own regulation."

The super studied his large, gnarled and powerful hands. They had been useful years back when he was a young constable working his beat. Hard times. Hard men to deal with.

"Well, the way I see it, it will be good for the section if he makes his mark, however he does it. It will have to be plain, old-fashioned police work then, won't it? Might give the lads here something to think about."

Moore nodded. He knew his man. "And your other reason?"

"I never did like those damn boys in the white coats." He saw his deputy's quizzical stare and added forcefully, "Well, dammit, it's too mechanical, isn't it? The machine does all the critical work. Trial and error, all down the line. Nobody sweats, or gets hungry or cold, or his face bashed or his head bonked while he's at the job. You get the picture I'm drawing, Amos?"

"Yes, sir. Sounds a bit like yourself."

Twenty-Three

That afternoon, the detail men were out on the golf course poking into the thick gorse and bracken and trampled-over grass. One of them exclaimed sharply, as he leaned down, "Here, now what's this?"

"What's it look like?" his companion officer said.

"A bloody 5-iron, is what it is. Look here, see all the red marks."

"Aye, I'm not that blind, O'Grady."

"Well, now, what do you think?"

"I'm thinking they'll have you in for the murder, man."

"How's that?"

"You picked it up, dumb sod. Now you've got your own prints on it."

"Well, how was I to know if it was the murder weapon before I picked it up to see?"

"You tell that to them, son. I'll be with you for the laughs."

Twenty-Four

The Chief Superintendent was sharpening his pencil with a jackknife when his deputy Moore came in. Shavings were all over the desk. There was a pencil sharpener handy but Amos Moore knew better than to suggest his chief's using it. It's got to be the old-fashioned way, how he did it as a boy. Otherwise you're only wasting your breath on him.

"Now there's a proper point for you," the big man said proudly.

"Aye, it is that."

"Notice the thickness, Amos. Got all the lead I want. The damn machine there won't give it to me, now will it?"

Well, what's it matter? Moore thought. If it don't work out right, so you give it another whirl. Better than having your desk and pants all covered with the stuff. He waved a paper. "They've found the murder weapon down at Rosslare. A 5-iron, it was."

The chief was twirling the pencil, admiring the point from all angles. "Mashie, they called them in my day. What's your thought on it?"

"The girl's face was battered in with it. Series of severe blows. I would say a personal affair, not political." Well, that part's a relief anyway. If they get through the next round without a casualty, I'll be happy. They had to be out of their minds to bring all those bigshots down there together. But I suppose golfers are all mad, to begin with.

The chief had placed his sharpened pencil carefully to the side, and now he picked up another and began hacking at its bottom with sharp, confident strokes of his big knife. "They've got good wood on this one," he said. "See how uniform the shavings are." Moore looked but didn't venture an opinion. He couldn't see any difference. Same mess, he thought. "I'll tell you what I think," Gallagher continued. "They'll now be finding the poor man who reported the club missing from his bag. They'll find his prints on the club, and hold him for interrogation."

"Golfers are always losing clubs, aren't they? There's always stacks of them in the Lost and Found. Man makes his shot, leaves his club on the ground, and forgets where he put it."

Gallagher was blowing the carbon dustings off his new pencil point. Christ! thought Moore, now he's got black all over his shirt and tie, part of his face. Why can't he use a pen, like the rest? "Now there's a point that will last me," Gallagher said. "You can't say the same for those blasted ballpoint pens, can you? They're always running dry."

"Aye," Moore said. "You're dead right on that, sir."

Twenty-Five

Stanwood was halfway across the dining-room to his table when the affable headwaiter Doyle intercepted him. "Your pardon, sir, but the lady in the corner, Miss Garner, asked me to stop you if I could. She'd like your company at her table for dinner."

He turned. She waved, beckoning, smiling. Why not? he thought. Your thoughts tonight will only curdle your stomach. Might as well be with someone pleasant.

"I don't like eating alone," she said. "And you did treat me to Mrs. McSwiney's meat pie this afternoon. So this is my treat, if you have no objection."

Stanwood shrugged and sat down. "How can I object? You're beautiful and easy to be with." Is that me saying that, he thought. What's come over you, Billy boy?

She let her head fall back and laughed. "You sure you're not Irish? You have the blarney or are getting it fast, that's certain."

He shook his head. "As a matter of fact, I was questioning my words to myself. I'm not given to making extravagant statements."

"Wonderful. Then that gives it more solid meaning." She handed him the menu. "I'm having a drink, and then the soup and fish. The Rosslare trout is very good here."

"I forgot. You did say you come here often."

"For years and years. It's like a home away from home, this hotel. They spoil you rotten with all the good food." Noticing his eyes and thoughts had shifted inward again, she impulsively reached across the table and lightly pressed his hand. "I'm terribly sorry. I keep forgetting your mind has to be occupied with the terrible thing this morning."

He wagged his head. "It's true, but I have to get my mind off it some time. It's one of the reasons I accepted your offer to dine with you. You lighten my miserable mood."

"Well, then, just one question, and we'll try to put it aside during dinner. What happened later when you went off with Paddy Moran? Did you unearth anything about Noreen?"

"Nothing. Or as her stepfather Matt Bogson kept saying, 'Nowt'. Comes to the same thing, I guess. Mrs. Kelly seems confined to her chair, and doesn't move a finger."

"How awful!"

"Yes. But even more so is her feeling about her daughters. Kate, dead last year, and Noreen, who was murdered she knew, earlier this day."

"You shouldn't be surprised," she said. "You know a mother's feelings – "

"Not this one's, I didn't. She didn't have any. Nothing. Nowt, as the man said. No sadness, no sorrow, no tears. It was incredible."

Her eyes were wide with shocked disbelief. "I can't believe it."

He shrugged, and seeing a waiter nearby, beckoned him over and ordered his drink. "When I mentioned Katie dying, it was more of the same; no interest. Believe me, Mary, I would willingly have strangled her where she sat. And the man with her. A duplicate copy giving me more of the same. For all they admitted to me, Noreen grew up invisible. Nobody knew her or saw her, she had no friends, boys or girls. For reasons best known to themselves, Mrs. Kelly either hated her daughters, or resented them enough to pretend neither of them ever existed."

She sat speechless, her eyes soft with concern. Finally she said, "You don't think it's the shock of the event, do you? Sometimes it takes something horrible like that to turn one's senses completely off or askew."

"Not really. I thought about it, but no, I don't. As a matter of fact, the only time Matt Bogson showed any emotion was when he walked me to the door. He couldn't have me leave without knowing he was a wealthy man. Said he owns all the caravans around, and the land, as well. I imagine it might break him up a little if one of them develops a leaky roof, or something goes wrong with the plumbing."

"Those little trailer huts, you mean, that are all

around?"

"I guess so. Back home, we call them trailers. Mobile homes. Some are fixed to the ground, others travel on wheels. I suppose these here are the permanent kind."

She looked blank. "I wouldn't know. It's terribly disappointing to meet that kind of response, Bill. But you can certainly ask around. You're bound to find people who knew Noreen. Or don't you have that much time?"

He smiled tautly. "That's different. It happens to be the one thing I've lots of. And I may be travelling up to Belfast soon. The old man, Bogson, hinted that she might have been in some kind of trouble up there. Maybe I can find out what that was about."

"But surely you have to stay here, at least until you find the murder weapon, how she was killed?"

Stanwood shook his head. "The police will be going over every inch of the golf course, and the beach beyond. All that rough grass. It could be hidden for a long time, but it's not too important, really."

Her eyes showed surprise. "But I thought that was always the key. The way you detectives worked."

"Not at all. What's important is to find the kind of person who would kill her that way."

She repressed a shiver. "I don't understand. Wasn't it the usual, if you'll pardon me, blow with a blunt instrument?"

"The police surgeon in Wexford probably has finished his autopsy by now. He'll find the probable causes of death, the fatal blow to the head, internal bleeding, exposure. But I'm more interested in the way she was killed, you see."

"The way? Do you mean, whether struck from be-hind, caught by surprise?"

"No. In any event, she wasn't struck from behind. It was a direct frontal blow, followed by a series of blows.

It was a very savage attack. Regardless of the prints the police find, the murderer left his own imprint for me to follow. It's a special type of killer."

"I'm afraid this is getting to be too much for me. I don't understand – "

"It's the way she was assaulted, you see. Whoever killed Noreen Kelly either hated her or feared her very much."

They sat in silence for a moment. The waiter came up and asked if they were ready to order. She looked at Stanwood and he nodded. "I understand the Rosslare trout is very good here."

"Aye, that it is, sir."

"Fine. Make it two of them." He turned to look at her. "You wanted the soup, too?" She nodded mutely. Stanwood handed the menu back to the waiter. "Two of the same all around." He raised his empty glass. "And the same here."

She stared at him. "After all you said, I'm surprised that you can eat."

Stanwood shrugged. "I've been through it before. After the grief, it gets to be interesting."

Twenty-Six

I've scared bloody hell out of her, and that's a fact, Stanwood thought later. If I see her again, I'll have to remember to keep it light, and not go into the gory details.

He could still see the shock in her eyes, her face losing colour as he described the blows to Noreen's head. She ate listlessly afterward, and when he realized what effect his words had and apologized, she only shook her head, saying it was not his fault at all, and that a sudden headache had come on.

"Sure, and I'm the one gave it to you."

When they left the table, she asked if he would join her in a walk along the beach. But Stanwood pleaded off, insisting he was poor company, and the cool night air would be better for her head without him. She had her heavy sweater on the chair, and he helped her on with it, walked with her to the outside terrace door, and said goodnight.

As he approached the reception desk, he was happy to see the girl there who knew the Kelly family, sitting at her desk going over accounts. "Sheila," he said, and she jerked in her chair as if stricken. Her eyes brimmed with tears.

She ran toward the counter dabbing at her eyes. "Oh, you poor man. Here you've come all this way only to find her dead. Was it you who first got the sad news this morning?"

He patted her hand, trying to calm her. "Yes. I guess it's bad for you, too. You knew her and the family. How did your mother take it?"

"Just terrible, sir. The Nolans are all cry babies, and she's been like me all through the day. I just left her a little back at the house."

"I suppose she was over to see Mrs. Kelly and offer her sympathies."

"That she did, sir, early on."

"I was over there myself. I hope she got a better reaction than I did."

"What do you mean, sir?"

He looked intently at her. "Last time we spoke, you were kind of hinting to me that something was wrong at that house. I'm still trying to understand it. Mrs. Kelly was bearing up as if nothing had happened. Was it the same for your mother?"

"I don't know, sir. I didn't ask."

"Is she crippled or what? She sat in her chair and didn't move a muscle."

"It must be the shock, sir, even though you're saying she acted like she didn't care."

"You're saying she can move?"

"Well, I haven't seen her in a long while, but I never heard much was wrong. Perhaps since Mr. Kelly died, it's come over her."

"It's possible," he said. "But she didn't show any sympathy for Kate, either. Bogson was with her, and didn't look surprised, although he knew what I was talking about."

She smiled faintly. "Well, I'm sure there's nobody in town could give you a kind word for that one. He bullies near everyone in sight, and because he's so rich, he gets his way about it."

"Maybe. But he's not bullying Mrs. Kelly. The shoe's on the other foot there."

"I'm glad to hear that, sir." She had regained her composure now. "And will you be leaving us now, and going on home?"

"Not yet, Sheila. I've a little work to do here. Maybe you can help. I know Noreen didn't stay home when she came here. Do you have an address for her? Maybe if I went through her place, I might find out what happened here."

"I'll see if the hotel has anything in the employment file." She went to her desk, opened a drawer, and returned with a sheaf of papers. She turned the pages slowly, scanning the listing. "No, there's nothing for her here. She worked part time, you see, and knowing the owner of the hotel these many years, as she did, there was never a problem about Noreen's references. Whenever she came down from Dublin or Belfast, she might have stayed at any of the local bed and breakfast places, seeing it was only for a few days. It's cheaper, you see. Or then she may have stayed with friends."

"What friends? Can you give me some names?"

"Well, as I said, sir, Noreen and I weren't that close. The girls who work here come and go. Back to London, for better pay, or home again to their families in Ireland, Wales or Scotland. It's nearly season's end now and they'll be off soon again. I don't know any girl here she was close to."

"All right. What about boy friends? An attractive girl like her had to know some men."

"I don't doubt it. I've seen the single men here, and the married ones, too, take a good look at her when she came by. But the only boy I've seen her with on her visit this time is Mickey Muldowney."

"Muldowney? He wouldn't happen to be driving a small yellow car, would he?"

Her eyes sparkled. "The little Honda. How did you know that, sir?"

"I saw her get in it the day I arrived. Does Muldowney live in Rosslare?"

"That I don't know. He could have driven down from Dublin or elsewhere to see her, you know. There's another smaller hotel here you might check. Golfers Inn. Or you might ask the manager of the caravans up the road. That's Mr. Zale. He visits our bar here nights. He would know more than I."

"I thought people rented the caravans for long periods."

"Some do. But if there's a vacancy, Donald Zale will put you up. Mr. Bogson likes the idea of money coming in, you see." She pointed to a painting on the wall. "That's one of Donnie's. He's an artist but needs the job to make a living."

Earlier, Stanwood had noted absently the paintings and prints on the walls of the corridors. They looked first-rate, of museum quality, and this one the girl was pointing out seemed equally good. A colourful landscape in watercolour. Stepping closer, he saw it was a scene recalling the local golf course. "Not bad," he said, "but then I'm no judge." He was writing swiftly in his pocket memo-book. "What about the owner of this hotel? He might have some background on Noreen."

The girl shook her head. "Mr. Shannon owned the place, like his family before him. But he died a while back, and now it's Mrs. Shannon who runs the Strand. But she's off to France with her two daughters on a vacation."

"When do you expect her back?"

"In about two months. She left just before you came, sir."

Stanwood scratched his head. "I doubt that I'll be around that long. Would you know what school Noreen went to here?"

"There's just the one. Down the road by the golf club. One of the sisters there will remember her."

"Wonderful. I'm glad I finally found somebody who knows everybody here."

"I know some, but I'm only here again the past year. It's working in London I've been. And I'm back only because my mum isn't too well. She's getting on, and my dad is gone, so it wouldn't be right for me to stay away no more."

"That's too bad. You're a good girl to be thinking of her now instead of your own life."

"Oh, there's time for mine. I'm in no hurry. Whatever is in store for me can wait a bit longer."

Stanwood nodded, smiling. He wanted to ask more questions. About Mary Garner, for one. An attractive woman like that, coming back to this hotel many times, as she had told him, surely she must have made many male friends. The guests came back here, as she did, year after year. Wasn't it the headwaiter Doyle who had told him that? And where were her friends? She seemed alone each time he saw her.

"Anything else, sir, before I go back to my account books?"

Stanwood was leaning on the counter, his absent gaze fixed on the wall mirror. "Just one more, Sheila. Are there any guests here down from Belfast?"

"There was just the one, I remember."

"Could you give me his room number?"

"Well, sir, he's gone now. Checked out."

"Can you tell me when?"

She turned to the file cards. "Friday afternoon late, it was."

Noreen had been killed some time between 10 o'clock that evening and shortly before dawn. Was it the Belfast guests who had frightened her? "I'd like his name. His Belfast address, too, please."

"Tomas Desmond is his name. And here's the card with his home address you'll be taking down."

He copied down the address, a number in Ben Madigan Road, Newtown Abbey, County Antrim, Northern Ireland. Is it possible, he wondered, the man is with the IRA? Down here to make a hit on the VIP group? That Noreen somehow got mixed up with that? His thoughts circled. That louse Bogson said she was wild, up and down from Belfast.

He checked his imagination. A bit far-fetched for now, he told himself. But if nothing develops here, I'll be calling on Mr. Desmond.

Enough for now, he decided, and thanking the girl, turned for the stairs. He saw the security guards at intervals along the corridors, one against the wall near the stairs. Their eyes met, the man inspecting him casually, nodding before his eyes went blank.

"Evening, sir. Had yourself a good dinner, did you?"

"Rosslare trout. Fish the way it ought to be. Well, good night."

At his door, he realized his key was not in his pocket, but had been dropped off at the reception desk for convenience.

He was berating himself for forgetting, having to go down again. His hand was on the door. The latch clicked and the door swung open. Curious, he thought, walking in.

He checked the room and bath with the lights on, then stood looking out of the window. Had the maid doing his bed forgotten to lock the door behind her? Was it accidental? No matter, he thought. It'll give me something else to think about.

Twenty-Seven

Mr. Charles O'Hanrahan was sitting at home, watching the telly in his living-room, when his wife came in.

"It's Constable Rattigan, Charlie. Albert. He asks if he might have a word with you."

"What about?"

"He didn't say, dear."

"Well, then, ask him in."

"I did that and he says he'd rather wait out on the step."

O'Hanrahan looked at the telly and at the beer still remaining in his glass. This was a girlie show, one of the new T and A comedy series, and he hated to give up so much as a single moment of lechery. "What's young

Kevin been up to, do you think?"

"I don't know, dear. He's up in his room, if you want to ask him."

O'Hanrahan rose. "It'll keep. I'll speak to the garda first. And don't be changing the channel on me, I get a bellyful of laughs out of this show."

"I know, dear. If only you'll remember they're all a bit young for you."

"Aye, and don't I know it." He stomped to the hall and flung the door open. A light rain was softly falling. "What the hell are you doing standing in the rain, Rattigan? Come inside if you want to talk."

"I don't mind the rain. And if you don't mind, I'd like you to be sending out the boy to me."

"Kevin? What's he done?"

"Nothing, Charlie. I'm just asking you to send the lad out for a few words with me."

"Well, why the hell can't you come inside and talk where it's dry?"

The men were about the same age, had grown up together in the town, and knew all there was to know about one another. O'Hanrahan was a short, stocky man, a successful businessman. Rattigan, the garda, dour, thin and not going anywhere in his profession, and well aware of the fact.

"O'Hanrahan," he bellowed suddenly, "now if I wanted to come inside where it's nice and dry, as any man short of being blind or a fool could tell, then I would. But instead I'm standing out here in the rain and asking you to send the boy out. And I happen to know what show it is you're watching inside on the telly, and begrudging me any second you're not looking down those little colleens' dresses, so do as I ask, man, and get back to your favourite sport."

O'Hanrahan looked at him. "All right, Albert, I'm sending him out right now, and I'm hoping the heavens fall while you're talking to him out here. Christ, do I hate dumb coppers!"

Young Kevin, suddenly alert to the threatening tread on the stairs, managed to hide the worn girlie magazine he was lusting over, before his door was thrown open. He saw a look in his father's eyes that he interpreted as fatal indeed, if he did not rise at once. And so he did, knees trembling, although at twelve he was nearly as big as his dad, and perhaps in better condition.

"Well, what's up, dad?" Kevin said. "If you called, I didn't hear."

O'Hanrahan wagged his thumb ominously toward the open doorway. "Constable Rattigan is outside the door wanting to have a word with you."

"Out in the rain? Why didn't you ask him in, pa?"

O'Hanrahan unreasonably reached out, grabbed his young one by the scruff, and propelled him vigorously toward the steps. "I'll ask him in when I feel like asking him in. Now get out there and let him say whatever he's come to say. And when you finish, then you and I will have a little meeting on the matter. Right, son?"

"Why, sure, pa. I haven't done anything. Honest."

Halfway to the door, his mother stopped him. "And have you lost your mind, Kevin O'Hanrahan, going out into the rain without your coat?"

"It's okay, mum. Pa said to get out there to see Mr. Rattigan. He didn't say nought about wearing a coat. Anyway I'll be but a minute."

"Oh, did he not then? I'll have my own word with him on that." She turned from him, her voice rising. "Charles O'Hanrahan, have you gone daft?"

When Kevin opened the outside door, the rain was falling harder. He looked with youthful compassion at the soaking constable. "Gee, Albert, why are you standing out in the rain? Can't we talk inside where it's dry?"

Rattigan eyed the young sprout through the rain drizzling down his cap. He'd known the lad since he was born, and was godfather to him, as close to benign uncle as a man could ever hope to be. But the rain and the circumstances had changed a lot of that.

"I know the difference between wet and dry, Kevin. I was just after going through that with your father. Now close that door. Aye. And for this occasion, don't 'Albert' me or 'uncle' me. I'm here as an officer of the law, and if you don't tell me what I'm here to know, I'm taking you off with me and locking you up."

Kevin looked at the benign fellow he knew who had suddenly turned into a steely-eyed, unfriendly, water-loving minion of the law. "Gee, Albert – I mean, Officer Rattigan, what's it all about? I mean, I haven't done nothing."

Like an omen dropped from the skies, the rain began pelting down with sudden force, as if denying his words. Rattigan somehow sensing this miracle grinned evilly. "So it's nothing you've done, eh? And I suppose it wasn't you along with the pack of them doing your All-Hallows Eve parade the other night, tromping through the Strand grounds, scaring the people there half to death, you and the rest of your friends, whose names you'll be giving me, with the poor witch you'd found somehow and had tied to keep her in her torment."

Young Kevin, the innocent, gaped. "Saints, Albert! How'd you find out it was me?"

"I've got me ways. I been with the garda long enough to do simple detective work. If anything happens in Rosslare that Kevin O'Hanrahan isn't a part of, I've not yet seen the day." There was an ominous roll of thunder. Kevin flinched, rain-sodden and unhappy. "Are you ready to give me the names of all them that was with you?"

"Well, sure. We didn't do anything. There was me and Dinny and Kathy and Shamus and – "

Rattigan trying to keep track of the confession with ball point and ever-ready notebook found out he was making blurred notes he would never be able to read back.

"I tell you what, Kevin. You go back up to your room now and write all them names down while they're still fresh in your mind. And when you're all done, you be bringing the list down to me."

"Okay, sure, Albert – I mean – " He was reaching blindly for the door knob behind him when the constable friend of other days leaned over him suddenly in a hideous growling voice.

"And what did you do with the witch, young Kevin? Are you forgetting that's why I'm here? Don't you know the witch is the one found dead the next morning?" As the boy stared up at him, Rattigan added, "Aye! Murdered, she was. Bludgeoned to her death, poor girl. Noreen Kelly, it was, one of our own lovely girls."

Kevin stared, wide-eyed, shaking. "But we let her go, Albert. Honest we did. We let her go right down near the school. She ran off onto the golf links."

Rattigan's voice retained its growling menace, with an added silkiness. "Oh did she now? Let her off, did you all? Not murdered the poor girl right there, did you not? Well, Kevin, my boy, you put all that down, too, while you're writing the rest, and when you're all done with it, I'll be taking it around to the other hooligans."

"What for, Albert – uh – Officer Rattigan? It's true like I'm telling you."

"What for, Kevin?" The rain-smeared face of Rattigan loomed dangerously close. "So there'll be witnesses to what you wrote. It'll be, near as make out, your confession, lad."

Kevin choked on the word. *"Confession?"*

The avuncular old friend was back. "That's right, Kevin my boy. Now you trot on up to your room and put it all down nice and in order." As the boy wheeled away from him, sobbing, he added, "And mind your father's hand on the way up!"

Twenty-Eight

Austin Kilty was the head professional at the Rosslare Golf Club. A burly, powerful man, he had been headed for a top tournament career when quite suddenly he was laid low by the affliction common to the game, dreaded by all who played, known as "My fucking sacro-iliac". He dropped out of tournament play when the worn-through discs refused to mend, and had to settle for a less glamorous life as a club professional. The osteopaths and the medics could do nothing for him, the back continued to plague him, and if he hadn't already been a drinking man, the condition would have driven him to it. He ran the pro shop and the course, and gave the obligatory lessons to the hackers and duffers who searched each day for the secret in vain. The secret for them, as Kilty well knew, was to get rid of the clubs, find another pursuit, but inasmuch as he was condemned to live his life as a suffering man, wracked by the spasms of nerve pain, he had decided to hold his tongue and let them all learn how to suffer, too.

This day had been a particularly trying one for him. Not so much for his chronic condition, but because the VIP tournament of international golfers had attracted a crowd, turning his normally quiet club into a carnival scene, and people he hadn't seen for years approached him, asking one after the other, "Well, Austin, how goes it with the back?"

He was sick of telling them how it went with his fucking back, and stoic that he was, fixing his concentration on the completion of this tournament next day, and then he wouldn't have to answer any more stupid questions. When a man has a bad back, everybody knows how it goes with it.

Now he saw he had more dumb questions to attend to. A group of policemen, headed by an officer in charge whose feet were obviously killing him, and good for him, thought Kilty, were holding a bloody golf club out to him, and asking if he had any idea who owned the bloody thing.

It took the merest glance for him to recognize the club, an Australian make of a top line, not common to the local golfers. He saw the grip immediately as one he had himself repaired for the man, and since the selfsame owner of the club had reported this particular 5-iron as missing from his bag, lost somewhere on the rotten course with its impenetrable clumps of high grass and attendant gorse, it was as easy as waking up stiff as a board and unable to tie his shoelaces for him to identify the golfer.

But Kilty had never been fond of coppers. As a youth, his first love tryst with Kathleen Hogarty in the back seat of an old Ford sedan had been interrupted by one with a flashlight. When the officer had passed on, after his ribald laugh and warning about speaking to Mr. Hogarty about this, the peak moment for love had sputtered out and gone. Kathleen was in tears, she wouldn't permit him to touch her again, she went off to school, she married another, and young Austin hated them all from that bleak lost moment on.

Now he looked at the club as if he had never indeed seen one before. "Hm, appears to be a 5-iron, does it not?"

"Says so right there. Number 5 on the bottom of the blade. Any idea whose it is?"

"They're all losing clubs here, you know. It's a frustrating course, and sometimes if they don't lose one proper, they throw one. Only when they settle down with their temper and try to find it, it's gone. Down somewhere in the rough."

"It says Australian-made here. Got any chaps here from that place?"

"Why'd they want to come here? It's a long trip just to lose a ball, or a club, for that matter."

"Now look here, Mr. Kilty, this here is a murder case that we're investigating. A local girl was killed with it."

"So I hear, and sorry indeed to hear about the Kelly girl. But you don't know for certain this was the instrument that did the killing, do you? Some bash their ankles on the way down and draw blood. Or hit at a rabbit that got their ball."

"Well, sir, we'd like to question the man." As Kilty hesitated, trying to recall how sweet it was in the back seat that one time with Kathleen Hogarty, before that big bastard came along the lane, the policeman with the club frowned, and added threat to the unction in his voice. "Now, sir, if you can't make the connection, we'll have to take all your records and receipts up to Wexford town and go over them there, and maybe we can find who was here from out of town and reported loss of this here particular club."

Kilty didn't want them going through his records. Next thing he knew, he could expect a suspicious query on the way he kept his books. Perhaps he was taking in a bit over the top, they might infer. Sometimes, he recalled, he did forget to enter a pound or two for a ball, or not write down the lesson fees which he collected in cold cash.

"I'll go through my book and see. Maybe it's something been reported to my assistant Padraig, when I was out. Hold on."

He was back outside in a while, pretending to read from the ledger. "There's a George Hanna, comes here from Galway to play. Plays here often. I see here the notation of the missing iron from his bag. Australian make, same line. Of course, you'll remember he's not the only one to use that make of irons. They're good ones and popular. It could well be some other chap from – "

The officer interrupted. "Where can we find Mr. Hanna?"

Kilty, defeated, pointed. "Out on the course. Should be about near the 17th by now."

Twenty-Nine

Dr. Brendan Devlin was the police surgeon at Wexford. He was a dapper, sprightly man belying his years, and out-going, fun-loving and jolly; in stark contradiction to his delegated profession, which consisted in the main of closely examining expired and sometimes brutally injured bodies at his feet.

He was intoning his most recent finding. "Death due to hypostatic bronchial pneumonia resulting from excessive blunt-force trauma of the right anterior portion of the head inducing subdural haematoma."

Detective Inspector Shaw had been giving up the better part of his sleeping habit of late, and found himself nodding. "Any other finding you can give us,

Brendan, expressed if at all possible in language
Goggin and I can understand?"

Devlin smiled cheerfully. "That limits me con-
siderably, John, but there is no way I can obfuscate the
fact of the girl being two months' pregnant."

"Write that down, Goggin. There's a word you can
spell." Shaw said.

Detective Goggin wrote dutifully, his hand neat and
decisive. "Pound to a pint our Yank didn't know that."

"He won't, unless you tell him."

The medical examiner closed his case with a metallic
snap. "I'll leave you boys to it. This one is easy. All you
have to do is find a left-handed fornicator with a
temper and passion for golf included."

Goggin sighed with relief. "Lets me out. Shaw
knows I don't play golf."

Shaw got to his feet. "Let's get on with it then."

He and Goggin left the room in tandem, crossed the
narrow hall and entered another larger room with desk
and chairs, peeling brown walls, and a nervous waiting
man.

"Sorry to keep you waiting, Mr. Hanna," lied Shaw.

"It's the nature of the business," Goggin added
sincerely.

George Hanna was a man from Galway, noted for
its scenic beauty and fierce, inclement weather. He was
a golfer, and, masochistic as the rest, had been coming
to Rosslare for many years to test his uneven skills on
the windswept, gorse and bracken-lined fairways of its
6495 treacherous yards.

Like most, he had lost too many balls in the
knee-high rough and grassy bunkers on most
occasions. This day had turned out to be the crowning
mockery of his life. For it was on the 476 yard 12th, par
5, when for the first time he could remember, he was
on the green, hole-high with his second, putting for an

improbable eagle, that he had been nabbed.

Flushed from his foursome late in the day by inordinately obdurate coppers, unsympathetic to his pleas to be allowed to putt out, he had been transported immediately to this hideous mockery of a room in the Wexford police station. Here he had sat for hours, alternating his thoughts between wondering what they had got him for, and if he would have made the eagle putt. Had he missed, he had at last concluded, jailing would be justified. In his heart, he knew life would never allot him another chance like that at Rosslare, where par is difficult, birdies rare, and the eagle unattainable by any man who can count.

Shaw observed the man gnawing his right hand fingernails and knuckles, rubbing his right cheek as if with incipient toothache, scratching his right ear, all outstanding feats of habit control for a left-handed man. The fatal blows, as the jolly ME had recently pointed out, had been a left-handed swing, judging from the victim's battered right frontal features, and now here was the damn culprit obviously right-handed. His immediate depression was suddenly lifted, when with the true detective's gift of recall, he remembered golf is supposedly a left-handed game.

That's it, Shaw rhapsodized internally, how many times have I seen the duffers swinging the club with their left arm in practice? To strengthen it, I've been told. So let him even pick his nose now with his right hand, it's all one to me.

Nevertheless, to table the matter securely once and for always, he asked, "Tell me, Mr. Hanna, are you right or left-handed?"

Hanna visibly shuddered. "There's no curse like being a left-handed golfer. The courses all favour the right-handed ones, if indeed favour is the word."

Shaw persevered. "Are you yourself then right or

left-handed?"

"Well, I'm right-handed. But it's a left-handed game, as you probably know."

Shaw nodded. "Yes, so I've – "

"The trouble comes right there at the onset. You're told to swing with the left, and of course, the left is weak as a kitten. I've had to work on it and work on it, constant practice, you see. But it was worth it. Now my left is strong enough to kill a man."

Shaw resisted the impulse to leap for joy. Proceeding cautiously instead, he asked, "Do you have any idea why you've been brought here, Mr. Hanna?"

Hanna, his lips pursed, assumed a thoughtful attitude. "Well, yes, I've given it thought. As you may have heard from your men, I was on that long par five with my second shot, not twenty feet from the stick. It was a sidehill putt on a fast slippery green – "

Shaw interrupted. "We're not concerned about the golf – "

Hanna cut him off. "But that's what puzzled me, you see. There was a chance I would make the putt for a three, giving me an eagle on the hole." He paused while Shaw looked at Goggin who returned his look, question for question. *What have we got here?* "But realistically, I didn't have a chance," Hanna resumed. "I've parred the bloody hole but once in ten years, never come near a bird, and here I am going for the impossible dream." He shook his head. "Truth is, if I'd taken the shot and missed, I'd probably killed myself, at least tried to take my head off with the putter. So I thought your men came along, assuming all that, to prevent my suicide and bloodying that miserable twelfth green."

Shaw was saved from nodding off by his associate prodding his ankle sharply with a heavy boot. "Yes, I see, yes, I see," he spluttered, trying to get back into

the game. His mind flashed back to his beginning days
at the Crime and Section primary school where one of
the enduring subjects was Queries and Other Criminal
Procedures. He sighed, reflecting that was all fantasy
and this at hand was the real world.

"Well, I'll tell you, Mr. Hanna, there's been a
murder and – "

"Must have been on the bloody fourteenth, right?"

Shaw checked his notes, nodding with full
satisfaction that he had them back on the track.

"Had to be the greenkeeper," Hanna said. "I'm
always in the bunker at the front of it. There's no way
of getting out of there without flying the green. It
doesn't hold. It's either a lost ball there in the gorse, or
you're out of bounds and it costs you two strokes.
Whoever tends that green deserves whatever they did to
him. After all, it's supposed to be a game, isn't it?"

Shaw looked at Goggin. Goggin cleared his throat.
Enough of this horseshit. "Mr. Hanna, where were you
on Friday night, All-Hallows Eve, between the hours of
ten o'clock and ten of the following morning?"

Shaw, listening closely, remembered that Dr. Devlin
had been his usual careful self when it came to
pinpointing specifically the exact moment of the crime.
"Approximately at midnight," he had said. "Eight to
twelve hours for rigor to set in, and the body was just
beginning to show the signs when discovered. Allowing
for temperature changes in the range shed, I would
assume within an hour or two of twelve midnight,
either way."

Detective Goggin, untroubled by his partner's inner
reflections, stayed doggedly with his query. "Well?
Please answer the question."

Hanna frowned, and seemed to be counting on his
fingertips. If he's counting them, Shaw thought acidly,
he'll soon discover he's got five on each hand.

Hanna cleared his throat and Goggin tightened his grip on the pen for speedy confession note-taking. "Friday night? That was last night. All-Hallows Eve, right?"

Shaw and Goggin nodded in unison to help the man along.

"Hours of between ten last night, then, and ten this morning? Today's Saturday, is it not? Or it was. Saturday night now?"

Again Shaw and Goggin showed the dual affirmative.

"Saturday, Saturday," Hanna said. "Friday night, from ten on. From ten on Friday night to ten this morning, which is Saturday."

Perhaps he's got a new mantra, Goggin thought. Those chaps from Galway would try anything.

Hanna laughed disconcertingly. "Well, that's a tough question, all right. The fact is, I honestly don't remember. I don't think I really did in the greenkeeper, but if I did, I've forgotten it."

He looked at Shaw and Goggin, in turn. "Seriously, did I really kill somebody?"

Goggin hated smart asses in general and in particular now, he hated this twat. Jesus, if you don't know whether or not you've killed somebody, what hope is there for the world?

"You're telling us then, to the best of your ability, you have no recollection of your activities last night?" Shaw said.

"Not for those hours, not from ten on."

"And previously to that?"

Hanna shrugged. "Friday night. I must have been drinking."

"You have witnesses to that effect, of course?"

"I do that. But then they were drinking, too."

I'm too old to be getting an ulcer, Goggin thought, or indeed am I? He looked at Shaw plaintively with an expression that clearly asked 'May I have the next question?'

Shaw nodded shortly and Goggin leaped in with it. "Do you know Noreen Kelly?"

A smile flashed instantly over the florid Hanna countenance. "I do, indeed. Lovely girl. Beautiful. Bright. Light on her feet. Not given to nagging." He paused and suddenly smote, as it was once earlier described, his forehead. "That's it!" he exclaimed, alive to the thought and beaming with total recall. "That's where I was. With Noreen. I was talking to her."

"About what time was that, sir?" asked Shaw.

"I can't remember. Kind of late, I guess."

"Perhaps you can remember where this alleged conversation with Noreen Kelly took place then?" Shaw said.

Head bobbing, Hanna snapped his fingers and said, "Out by the caravans, near the golf course. Near the 18th tee."

Goggin was rolling his eyes. "And then what happened?"

Galvanized into complete memory again, Hanna put his hand on his head, wincing at the touch and said, "Somebody bonked me over the head, knocking me out."

My missus comes from Galway, Goggin was thinking. It must be the winds and the tides. They're all daft. He looked at Shaw who had the worn appearance of a man poisoned to the gills, ready to drop off without a struggle. He's my partner, right or wrong, Goggin thought.

He funnelled his nasal voice directly at Hanna. "Perhaps you can tell us then how the girl was dressed when you saw her, Mr. Hanna?" He saw Shaw's eyes light up. There, I've saved the man again, but he'll be forgetting it in the hour.

The Galway man considered the question. He rubbed his nose with his knuckles. I'd like to punch it, Goggin thought. Hanna suddenly snapped his fingers. "Some crazy costume, it was. Terrible for a lovely girl like Noreen to be wearing."

"What sort of costume, sir?" Shaw said.

Goggin thought, The rotten bastard knows. He's having us on. He'll be snapping his blasted fingers again, watch.

Hanna snapped his fingers. Goggin nodded to himself. "That's it! A witch's costume, it was. For All-Hallows. You know, the mask and black hat, cape, long skirt, black shoes. I didn't recognize her at all, and she had to keep talking to remind me who she was. You ask her. She's got a good head on her, and will be remembering it was me."

Goggin and Shaw looked at each other, wondering what to do about this oddball, now that they had him. Maybe I can shut him up at least, Shaw thought, and said, "Mr. Hanna, Noreen Kelly is dead. Found murdered near where you say you last saw her alive."

Hanna blinked. Bit by bit he lost his colour. It was like watching a man turn himself into pasty wax. His lips pursed and he sucked air. Words tentatively forming in his mouth dissolved and returned to master control for refitting.

Goggin with his satyr's face watched clinically and without sympathy. The man's going to dissolve or explode, and I don't know which.

Detective Shaw sat tapping his pencil on his knee. He kept his eyes on his dangling foot, as if he had never seen it before from this angle. He had no reason to look at Hanna because he was never interested in process but only the final result.

Suddenly a great hoarse sound came from Hanna's throat. And to their amazement, he began to cry.

Thirty

In the starkly furnished interrogation room on Old Jail House Road, where frivolity was not encouraged, and serious questions asked over and again, sometimes repetitious, sometimes of no seeming consequence, with little regard for wounded sensibilities or nerves stretched to their utmost and threatening to burst their seams, the two detectives fired laserlike beams of inquiry into George Hanna's shrinking skull. Answers got, seemed of little help, bringing on as they did, only more questions. Once into the swing of it, detectives find it hard to shut themselves up. It's the rhythm of it. That and watching a man turn to jelly before their eyes.

"How long have you known Noreen Kelly?"

"About five years, maybe a bit more."

"Are you married?"

"Yes."

"Any children?"

"Three."

"All living with you in Galway?"

"Yes."

"What do you do for a living, Mr. Hanna?"

"Neckties. I manufacture neckties."

"And is that one of yours you're now wearing?"

"What? This is a sport shirt for golf. Doesn't take a tie."

"Sorry. Just checking to see if you know what a necktie is. (Haha. Don't worry. We'll nail the bastard yet.) "And where at do you make up these alleged neckties?"

"In Galway. Got a small factory there."

"And how long have you been coming to Rosslare?"

"Five, ten years."

"Which is it?"

"Closer to ten, I guess."

"And how long have you been in love with the deceased?"

"Five ... what? I never said we were in love."

"But you knew her well?"

"Fairly well. I mean, I always stay at the Strand. Saw her around. Passed a few jokes between us."

"Do you sell many ties down in Rosslare?"

"I come down to play golf. Who buys ties in Rosslare?"

"Wexford has stores. How about Wexford. Sell any there?"

"Not personally. I mean, perhaps a few orders come in from Wexford. Yes. Come to think of it ... "

"When did you first become intimate with the deceased?"

"Intimate? But I already told you ... "

"We're aware of what you told us, sir. How long have you been married?"

"Twenty years. Nearly twenty-one."

"How often do you come to Rosslare to play golf?"

"Once every year. About this time."

"Sometimes more often?"

"Well ... sometimes. That's rare. You see, I've my regular group to play with, my foursome and ... "

"How long do you stay each visit?"

"Seven days. A week, thereabouts."

"Sometimes longer?"

"Not as a rule. We come down together, leave together."

"Always?"

"Almost always. Sometimes I come down in my own car, if I've been off on a trip."

"Where might that be, sir?"

"Dublin. Belfast."

"Do some business there, do you?"

"They wear ties there. Why not?"

"And you met Miss Kelly up there?"

"What? Who said ... well, yes. But it was accidental. Just bumped into her. She worked the hotel there. I mean, she worked at it. In it."

"Which hotel was that one, sir?"

"Burlington."

"What about the one in Belfast?"

"She never told me about that one."

"But you knew she worked in Belfast?"

"Well, I'd heard ... but never found out where ... I mean, I never saw her there."

"And you spoke to her directly this past Friday night near the caravans?"

"What?"

"Near the 18th tee of the golf course."

"Oh. Yes. We spoke a few minutes before I got hit."

"Any idea who hit you?"

"No. It was dark."

"Any idea why you were hit?"

"No."

"What did you and the deceased talk about?"

"Nothing much. Small talk. Asked how I'd been. I asked the same."

"This while she was wearing the outfit of the witch?"

"Yes."

"You didn't ask why she was in it?"

"No. You don't ask girls why they're wearing this and that."

"And was that the only time you saw the deceased this visit?"

"Well, no. I saw her briefly once before."

"Where was that?"

"Saw her in the bar. We had a drink."

"And did the deceased tell you then she was pregnant?"

"What?"

"Is that why you killed her?"

"I never ... I never did."

"What was your relationship with the deceased?"

"We were friends."

"Did you ever go to bed with her?"

"Well, just the once ... maybe two times."

"You say you met Noreen Kelly in the lot by the caravans?"

"Yes."

"What were you doing there?"

"She called. Asked me to meet her."

"Where were you on taking the call?"

"At the hotel bar. There's a booth outside."

"Witnesses?"

"Yes, but I told you ... "

"Anybody see you leave?"

"Well, I can't swear to that."

"And you walked from the hotel two miles up the road to the caravans?"

"Well, yes, roundabout."

"Did you expect to meet Noreen Kelly there?"

"Yes. She asked me to be there."

"Do you have any idea why?"

"No."

"Do you have any idea who might have killed her?"

"She had other friends, you know."

"Can you give us their names?"

"There's this young chap Muldowney."

"First name?"

"Michael ... Mickey."

"Which?"

"I'm not sure."

"Anybody else?"

"Let me think."

"Where does Muldowney live?"

"Dublin, I think. Maybe near here. Waterford, perhaps. He's down often."

"How would you know that?"

"I've seen him about."

"You said young. What age is he?"

"Twenty ... twenty-five. Thereabouts."

"Have you recalled names of other friends yet?"

"Men or women?"

"Men first, please."

"There's a man in Belfast."

"Name?"

"Tug."

"That's his name?"

"Well, you asked me. That's all I know of him."

"Anybody else?"

"You might ask Matt Bogson, her stepfather. He'd know."

"All right, what about women friends?"

"There's the girl at the reception desk knows her. Sheila Nolan. And Mrs. Shannon the owner, and her two daughters, Linda and Nell."

"What about close friends, girls her own age she would have gone out with?"

"Down here? I can't think of any."

"Where, then?"

"She roomed with a girl in Belfast she told me. Kitty ... Kitty Mayo."

"The address?"

"Ben Madigan Road. Newtown Abbey."

"Phone number?"

"I ... I don't know it."

"When did you lose your golf club?"

"When? Last year, I guess."

"According to the records of the golf professional at the club, you claimed it was lost a month ago."

"I did? Oh, that one, yes. I'm in the habit of losing them, you see. I put it down and ... "

"Apparently this was an extra visit between your annual visits?"

"Well, yes, I suppose so."

"And did you see the deceased then?"

"No. She was supposed to meet me, but she never showed up."

"Was that fairly typical, would you say?"

"Yes, but I never blamed her. She's young, single ... I mean ... "

"Anything further you can think of, Goggin? No? Very well, then, Mr. Hanna, you're free to go. For the present."

"Thank you, gentlemen. You've been, uh ... very kind."

Thirty-One

"Well, what d'ya think?"

"Not our man."

"Lied a bit, though, don't you think?"

"Not much better at it than his golf, I'm thinking."

"You swallow that bit about meeting the girl out by the caravans and getting hit and knocked out?"

"Not half, I don't."

"You think he put her in the family way?"

"Maybe so, but don't think he'd be getting that right, either."

"For all the talk, we didn't draw much, did we?"

"Well, tomorrow's another day."
"Wonder how the Yank's doing."

Thirty-Two

Chief Superintendent Gallagher was buttoning his topcoat about to leave his office. It was dark outside, beginning to rain. Well, nothing new there, when didn't it? His deputy Moore entered waving a bit of paper with an air of excitement.

"Better see this before you go, sir. Just in from Intelligence Room."

Gallagher stopped poised, one button to go. "Give me the gist of it, Amos. The wife's having friends over for dinner, and I'll get bloody hell if I'm late again."

And who did not? Moore was thinking. He's a good man, top man. Only he hates to read reports. Always wants me to read 'em to him. Maybe he had a nanny read him bedtime stories when a toddler. "The Kelly girl, sir, the one found murdered down in Rosslare. Wexford sent up her prints. The girl has a record."

Gallagher sighed. He hated to stop at that last button. Would Mary understand? Did she ever? Should he call and wheedle an extra ten minutes out of her? No, he shouldn't, he decided, as he'd catch hell then for the call and more of the same later whenever he did get home. "What sort of record?" he asked, as if he couldn't guess.

"Dates back five years when she was caught running guns for the Provos. Did thirty days in Belfast Long Kesh. More recently she's been with a new group. Revolutionary Independents. IRI, they call it. They're the ones just bombed and sunk the British coal ship off

Coleraine, in Lough Foyle harbour."

"About the Kelly girl, you were saying."

"She and another woman are reported to be associated with Terry Dugan. He just got out of Maze prison up there. They're wanted for robbery of a Dublin-to-Belfast mail train, shooting a guard. Made off with three mailbags containing money and negotiable cheques."

"Did that, did she?"

"Yes, sir. It's all here and – "

"Well, she won't be doing it any more, now will she?"

"No, sir."

"Good night, Amos. If my wife calls, say I'm on my way."

Well, I'm not going to say no to that, am I? I'm not that crazy. Just overworked a bit. "Yes, sir. I'll do that. Enjoy your dinner, sir." Maybe with luck, I'll be out of here by midnight and find the cold pie waiting in the fridge.

Thirty-Three

"Telephone call for you, Mr. Hanna."

"What? I'll take it in the hall booth down near the bar."

"Hello. Is that you, Georgie?"

"Yes, say, who – is that you?"

"None other. Did they give you a bad time there?"

"Bad enough. I'm out of it now, I'm thinking."

"Tell them anything?"

"Only what I could."

"Careless of you to lose that club, now wasn't it?"

"Listen, I can't talk too long. My friends – "

"Well, I'm a friend, too, Georgie, am I not? You do remember me, George?"

"Yes. Now what exactly is it – "

"Will you be going on home soon, George?"

"I think so, yes. Few more days will end it."

"There is that possibility. How's your sense of adventure now? Blunted some, is it?"

"I think it is. Yes, to that. If it's what I'm thinking."

"That's not your strength, Georgie, thinking. Would you be interested at all in what I'm thinking?"

"I know you're always at it. But, listen, there's no more I can do."

"Pity. The girl was never meant for you, you understand that now?"

"I suppose you're right."

"There's more I'll be saying about it soon, Georgie. You may well count on that."

"I told you. There's no more I can do."

"Perhaps, George. Things change, and miracles do happen. You agree, do you not?"

"Yes. But I wish you'd see my side of it."

"What's to see? Has anything new been added?"

"Well, no, come to that."

"Ah, I thought as much. Now you will be careful, Georgie, will you not? I mean, especially careful."

"I guess I'll have to, won't I?"

"Indeed yes. And by the way, George, how's that head of yours?"

The phone clicked in his ears. It was not particularly cold there in the booth in the hotel corridor near the bar, but George Hanna could not repress a shiver. Odd thing, weather.

Thirty-Four

Stanwood got up Sunday morning and tasted the air. He couldn't remember doing that before. No more than he could recall waking up in a strange hotel room and wondering what he was going to do next. His mind took a strange circuit and he found himself wondering how it was in Wales on Sunday mornings, and what one would do next there. Like to see that school of hers, he thought. See how she does things. Bet the kids are crazy about her.

He swung his arms briskly and saw a big man in the mirror devoid of expression. Smile, he told his reflection. Where there's life, there's hope.

The VIP golfers had already left the dining-room for their match. Mary Garner was not at her table. A chunky little waitress gave him a big smile and a warming good morning, sir. He ordered breakfast. Oatmeal with the thick Rosslare cream, bacon and eggs, toast, coffee. When it came, he discovered that never in his life had he thought oatmeal delicious before. The bacon and eggs were like bacon and eggs. Stop stalling, he told himself, and get something going here.

He finished and went out the side door to avoid a chance meeting with the Garner woman. He wanted to check the caravan site and get to the golf course while the match was still on. There was still a possibility of violence. Noreen's murder could have been a separate event, or linked somehow to the international tournament. If he met the woman from Wales, his movements would be limited, perhaps sidetracked completely. If she's still around when I'm done, he thought, maybe I'll do something about that. And while you're at it, he added to his mental track, bear in mind you'll be running into a lot of competition for that one.

On his previous walk, he had noticed the old house with the Bed and Breakfast sign. They take lodgers, transients, he thought, maybe here's where Noreen bedded down the times she was here.

A sprightly, white-haired woman answered the bell on her door. "Yes, are you wanting a room? We'll be having one later today."

"Sorry, no." He explained his presence.

"Noreen Kelly? No, she's not been here with us."

He thanked her, went along the deserted main street. She had to bunk somewhere, he thought. If not at the caravans, then perhaps Muldowney knows. And let's not forget Tim Cullimore. He probably can tell me more than anybody here about her.

It was quiet at the caravan site. He counted roughly ten of the white trailers. Nothing stirred. Maybe at nine in the morning they're still asleep, or at church, he thought. Might as well look in at the golf match, and come back here afterward.

The tournament golfers were off to an early start again. Cars were jammed in every possible space in the lot, some overflowing, parked on grassy areas behind the near teeing sites. He hurried on to the course, noting again that the spectators were out ahead following the match.

More familiar with the course now, he took out his score-card and studied the diagrammed layout on the back. They were out past the fifth tee now. Ahead on the grassy bluff fronting the sea was the ranger's maintenance hut. He saw a guard stationed there. He cut across the rough, unwilling to come any closer to the shack with its grisly memories. They've probably checked the interior by now for prints, he thought. Again on his mental retina, he could see the lawnmower in the dark corner, the open bags of fertilizer, the cans of fungicide chemicals for weeding, rot-curing, recalling immediately the acid scent, the dry mustiness of the seeds and grasses spilling from their bags, the dried, darkened pool of blood. There were the gardening implements, the rakes, hoes, shovels and shears.

He shook his head, moving on rapidly. It didn't really matter which, if any, of the tools there had been the bludgeoning weapon. It was the mind of the murderer uppermost in his thoughts, the idea behind the person who would kill that forcefully and brutally. Let the Irish detectives take their prints, as he himself, or his men, would have done on a similar case. His method now would have to be more direct, more personal. Who could have done the thing?

He heard applause ahead from the spectators. He could see the thin crowd of onlookers trailing along the next four holes parallel to the sea. There was definite protection and security today. On nearly all the grassy knolls, bluffs or hillocks, stood solitary guards carrying weapons. That's better, he thought, they can spot any troublemaker in time from those hills.

He studied his card again. Directly across was where the action would be taking place, as the golfers made their turn to the ninth hole, heading in. The holes for the incoming nine were inland, far across from the sea, running close and parallel to the main street of Rosslare. There were a few houses there behind the rough and trees, and no spectators. It seemed sensible to head across and have some vantage point before the crowd poured down. Then he could keep in step with the golfers as the holes swung outward again for the final few finishing holes.

He soon found it was impossible to cut straight across the fairways. The rough grew all around, dense thickets, clumps of trees, knee-high grass, twisting paths of stone, dirt and gravel. He had to swing in a circular path to make his way, trotting around each new impenetrable thicket or bunker he came to.

The 12th hole, the centre of the golf course, was the point he aimed for. Not too far from the clubhouse, and if he had seen enough, it made for a shorter walk back to the hotel.

It took longer than he had thought. He heard the rippling of applause as he neared the 12th green. The advance foursome had made the turn at the ninth. They were hitting off the 10th, a short hole of 160 yards. The crowd was running ahead to see them tee off at the eleventh. He checked his diagram again. The green to the 11th hole was close to the teeing area of the 12th.

All that scurrying run for nothing, he thought. They'll be boxed in by the time they're on the green, and I'll miss it again.

He found another grassy knoll, climbed it. The golfers were coming straight down the fairway. The crowd had thinned out, trudging along the parallel rough. Dammit, he asked himself, which way do I jump now?

There was another small knoll not far off. He was nearly up it when he saw behind it a little yellow car parked in a lane. His mind flashed back to the first day he had seen Noreen. It was raining then, he hadn't seen the car clearly. A Honda, the receptionist Sheila had told him. Belonging to the light-haired youth he had seen. Mickey Muldowney, she said.

He was thinking of this, wondering if it was the same car, when he caught the dazzling reflection of sunshine, the glint on metal. His mind detached. Where the hell is the security force? There was a loud report. Somebody screamed on the fairway. He looked to see if anybody had been hit. A pack of people had converged in the centre of the fairway. There was a grinding clash of gears. He saw a blur of yellow car. It continued racing through the copse, and then it disappeared beyond the trees and he heard it humming down the road.

Stanwood didn't know it then, and never found out until he got back to the hotel, that the golfer down in the centre of the 11th fairway was Sir Rodney Clark, British Under-secretary of Finance, playing to a handicap of 6.

Not to worry. Sir Rodney was sorely hurt but not seriously, with a shoulder flesh wound. His right arm, as it happened, not the all-important golfer's left. Both he and his partner Cedric Rutledge were 2-up at the time in their match.

PART THREE
Thirty-Five

Mickey Muldowney was listed in the hotel phone directory. Simple as all that. Christ, he asked himself, are you sure you were a detective? He called the number, heard the ringing and hung up after a dozen. If he did it, he won't be in, if he didn't, there's no reason to be in, and if he didn't, then who did? So goes it in the deductive game.

He had Paddy Moran's card and called him at home. "More trouble here," he said. "Can I get you out?"

"The telly's on the bonk, and I can't watch the football. I'll be there as soon as I find me cap."

Stanwood was outside when Moran drove up. "Twenty minutes. That's not bad at all with the Sunday drivers about."

"I appreciate this, Paddy. We're looking up Mickey Muldowney. Can you find this address?"

"That will be Enniscorthy, outside Wexford. Not far. They've a nice museum. And what happened this day to stir you up so?"

"One of the golfers was shot during the match."

"Was the man Irish or English?"

"What's the difference what he was?"

"Well, sir, we don't shoot many of our own."

129

"The shot came from a car like Muldowney's, the small yellow car. Girl at the hotel said he drove a Honda."

Moran spat tobacco juice derisively. "Another of them little Japan bugs. But the damn car runs good. Cheap, too. There's lots around."

"Even if he's in the clear, I still have to ask some questions. Noreen was getting into his car, the last I saw of her alive."

"That don't mean nothing, sir. Down here, you grab a ride if it's going your way."

"Let's find out anyway."

"You're doing this on your own, then, not taking it to the Wexford coppers?"

"Not yet, anyway."

"Might be just as well. I had me talk with McSwiney last night. He'll be speaking to Tim Cullimore for you. Could be you'll learn something more about the girl."

"About time, too."

They were making good speed on the highway despite lanes thick with cars. "It's not only the Sunday drivers and the tourists out today," Moran said. "There's been talk of a petrol strike and people are getting around now to make their calls while they can."

They skirted Wexford and soon approached a smaller village. Moran looked again at the address Stanwood had written down. He swung the big Rover into a narrow lane, turned into a wide drive-way and stopped scratching his head. "My fault entirely, sir. The car didn't want to make the turn, but I did. It's the other side." He backed out, went ahead over a hill, and turned into a small side street. "There it is, sir. Shop on the corner. And there's your little yellow car, to the side."

The shop featured a weatherbeaten sign. AN-TIQUES. The door was closed and shuttered but

Stanwood didn't bother going toward it. He strode to
the car instead, putting his hands on it. He felt the
radiator, the hood, and then ran his fingers, kneeling,
over the tyres. He backed off looking puzzled.

"What's wrong, Mr. Stanwood?"

"The car's cold. Hasn't been used for hours,
certainly not today." He looked around, then at
Moran. "Do you know of a Honda dealer in Wexford?
New or used cars." Moran nodded and he got into the
Rover. "Let's go. Step on it."

"I thought you was going to ask Muldowney the
questions."

"They can wait. Go, man."

As the car turned about, blinds drawn over the shop
door were parted, and troubled blue eyes stared out.
Stanwood neither knew nor cared about this. But
Mickey Muldowney, on this Sunday morning, had to
wonder about it. He had a cold, his head hurt, and the
big man checking over his car looked like a copper.

Thirty-Six

"Tubby lady. Good size. Red hair, she had." The
Honda dealer in Wexford, Travis MacMenamin, was
describing the woman who had taken his car on a
trial-run demonstration. "I tried to tell her she was too
big for it, but she wouldn't pay me no mind."

Stanwood was checking the radiator, the bonnet, the
tyres, a ritual with him lately, it seemed. They felt cool,
but not that cool. He had a thought. "Did you check
the odometer before she took it out?" The dealer
nodded assent. "How about the mileage on it now?
Would you give me the figures?"

"Aye. She put thirty-two miles on the car."

"Twenty miles approximately to here and Rosslare

and back?"

"Aye."

The Honda was circumspectly clean, not a visible speck or blemish on it. "When did she take the car?"

"Late last night, it was. Near closing time, before ten."

"Ever seen her before?"

Headshake negative. Expression likewise. Hands, too. All of MacMenamin had never seen the lady before.

"Isn't it a bit unusual to let out a new car overnight?"

"We do it at times, sir. Got to check it out with the old man and the kiddies, and so on. Left a good deposit, she did. And washed it off before driving it back in. No harm done."

Stanwood didn't hold his breath on the next question, although he well might have. It was important. "When did she bring it back?"

"Not ten minutes ago, sir. Told me how sorry she was about it. Smiling all the while. Silly old bitch."

"Do you have a carwash near here?"

"Down the corner. Kilmore's. Right side. By the quay."

"Let's go, Paddy." About to step into the Rover, he stopped suddenly. "I'm sorry, Mr. MacMenamin, but this car will have to be impounded by the police. Don't let anybody touch it."

"Impound it? But it hasn't done anything!"

"It's been to Wexford and back, perhaps. Somebody in a car like this tried to kill a person there."

"Not this old cow. Not likely by half."

"When you call the police, ask for Detective Shaw or Goggin."

They left MacMenamin to his rueing and drove to the wash.

"I understand you just did a wash job on a new Honda. Yellow."

"Aye. Not long past. Anything missing? Car mat, maybe?"

"No. Show me the bin where you dump what's vacuumed out, swept off the floor, gravel from the tyres."

"More a barrel than a bin. Lost an earring, did she not? Well, likely you'll find it in there." As Stanwood walked to the metal barrel, the proprietor chuckled. "You'll be remembering today as your own lucky day."

"Why's that?"

"It's a fresh barrel. Nothing else in it but what's from the Honda. Our only wash so far today. Otherwise, man, you'd be dipping in over your elbows."

Stanwood tipped the barrel to its side, reached in and extracted a handful of dirt, grass and gravel. He found an envelope in his coat pocket, and dumped his findings in. He closed the fold, replaced it in his pocket, placed the barrel upright again and wheeled it aside.

"Save this for the Wexford police. Nothing else goes inside. What's your name, sir?"

"Kilmore."

"Much obliged to you, Mr. Kilmore. You may be an important witness for the police. Can you describe the lady who asked for the carwash?"

"Are you daft? All we do here is wash the cars."

"Try, please, Mr. Kilmore."

Kilmore reflected. "Built like a barge, she was. Bright red hair on her. Nose with a knuckle on it. Not bad legs, though, considering all."

Moran, laughing, turned to Stanwood. "Where next?"

"Muldowney. Maybe he's up by now."

Thirty-Seven

Muldowney had a nice shop in front, a comfortable apartment in the back, and a beautiful cold upstairs in his head. When he opened the door to Stanwood and Paddy Moran, his first thought was, Christ, they've got me at last. Ordinarily, his mind would have leaped to improvised scenarios establishing his innocence regarding this or that; but when a man is wrapped and shivering in a wormy bathrobe, his throat raw, his nose stuffy, his eyes watering, his chest barking at him as the virus steals sneakily about, he is not given to mundane thoughts such as arrest. Maybe with luck, I'll infect them both, he thought, and we'll all die happily in the front parlour. "Come in, gents," Muldowney said through his nose. "I assume you're not buying. The parlour's right behind the curtain."

"This is Mr. Moran. I'm William Stanwood." He disliked the antique dealer at once, knowing there was no way now that he could strike a man in that miserable sniffling condition. "Noreen Kelly was my sister-in-law. I came over to Ireland to see her, and did just the one time, Thursday. Did she tell you?"

"When would she tell me? She's dead now, you know."

Snotty little bastard. "She might have told you after she got into your car. This past Thursday, after noon, in the rain." Ignore those facts, if you can, Muldowney.

"No, that's right. I picked her up then. But she didn't say anything of your coming." He dabbed a soggy handkerchief to his red nose. "Have they found the murderer yet?"

"Not unless I'm talking to him now. That's okay. You're entitled to jump a little. As far as we know, you might be the last person to see her alive."

"You're wrong there, sir. I didn't do it, never. And after I dropped her off in Wexford, somebody else saw her then."

"Where did you drop her?"

"She wanted her hair done. There's a shop there on Slaney Street. The House of Scissors, it's called."

"And did you pick her up there when she was done?"

"She wasn't there. Girl inside told me she never did the job. Noreen suddenly ran off. That's all I know."

"Ran off after you left?"

"That's about right. I needed some petrol, and then was going to have my car checked. I had an hour to get back, you see."

"You never heard from her or saw her again?"

"No, sir. Anyway, I've been right here nursing my cold."

"How long have you known her?"

"How long? All her life. Noreen and I went to school together."

Did you kill somebody you've known since childhood? Stanwood wondered, or wait until you'd been married a few years. "Did you love her, intend to get married?"

"Well, yes, of course I loved her. But we were never to be married. She understood that. I've another girl in Dublin. And Noreen knew others, too. She only came back the past week. She's been up north mostly the last five years."

"I understood she left home three years ago when Matt Bogson moved in."

"You were told wrong. Noreen was gone before the man came. She did come back to see the old lady sometimes, or friends here, me included, some others in Wexford town."

"How did she get along with her mother?"

"It was mutual, sir. They hated each other. The old woman's a fanatic, you know. Drove poor Mr. Kelly out of his mind till he up and died."

"You may be right. I was there. Tell me, can Mrs. Kelly walk, get around? Or is she confined to the chair?"

Muldowney began to laugh, turned it into a racking cough instead. "She can walk when she wants to. The rest is for punishment."

"Punish who – for what reason?"

"Whoever is there, for whatever reason. She'll sit in the chair and not move, not talk, either. That's her punishment. If you want her down, all you need do is something you know the old lady don't like."

"Why do you think Noreen was killed?"

"She expected it. She was in a dangerous business, you see."

There you are, I told you, Stanwood said to his critical self. That accounts for the look I saw. So I wasn't imagining things. "What kind of business?"

Muldowney hesitated. "It will come as a surprise to you, sir."

"No more than her being murdered. Let's have it."

Muldowney sighed. "Mind if we have a bottle to go with it?" Stanwood nodded, and Muldowney sneezed and tottered off to the rear, disappearing in his kitchen. He came back with a bottle and three glasses. He poured his own, set the bottle between Stanwood and Moran, lifted his glass, drank it neat, said "Cheers!" belatedly and had a brief coughing spasm. Stanwood and Moran used the bottle to their own measurements until the youth uncoughed himself. He looked at Moran and then back to Stanwood.

"Moran's okay. Anything you have to say."

Muldowney brought a box of thin paper napkins closer. "It goes back a long way," he began. "You've heard no doubt of the IRA, the revolutionary party, the Provos?" Stanwood nodded. "Noreen joined up with them about five years ago. Soon after she left Rosslare. She was just a kid, tried Dublin for more fun, and that led to Belfast and real excitement. The trouble was, Noreen liked the fun and excitement, the idea of being with a gang, even to carrying a gun, but she never liked the killing.

"So she got out of that, and they liked her well enough to let her go. Then she joined another smaller group, the ISA, Irish Socialist Army. They were going to do it by more peaceful means, but before long, they got into scrapes, had to shoot their way out, and there she was again, carrying her big gun, not wanting to use it. She got out of there, and this year joined up with the IRI."

Moran interrupted. "Sure and I've never heard of that one meself."

"It's a new splinter group. Irish Revolutionary Independents. They had a more practical idea. Concentrating on getting money, instead. Robbing mail trucks, mail trains, banks. This was more to Noreen's liking. Running with a gang, making the plan, carrying it out, I guess it was all like living her own TV series. You know, the shoot-'em-up flicks.

"But again, like with the others, they ran into trouble. Had to shoot up a guard on a mail train from the Belfast run to Dublin, and then tried it again as a surprise on a return trip and they killed a train man."

"How do you know she never shot anybody?" Stanwood said.

"She told me, for one thing. And that's probably what got her killed down here, for the other."

"How's that?"

"The gang are all in for it now, wanted for murder, and they wanted her to be equal part of it. Killing and all, if need be. So she was sent down here to do a job. In good faith, you can say."

"On the golfers – the International tournament?"

"That's what she told me. It didn't matter who. Anybody at all. Dugan told her she could take her pick."

"Dugan?"

"Terry Dugan. Leader of the IRI. And I think he was down here himself this past weekend."

"Did she tell you that?"

"No, but when she ran out the hotel that day, Thursday, she was white. Scared stiff. She wouldn't want to give him away."

"Why would he expose himself, take a chance like that, coming down to Rosslare, for anybody to see? He's wanted, isn't he?"

"The group is new, as I said. And Terry Dugan's face isn't that known yet. But Noreen was his special pet, you see, and so it was up to him to make sure she did the job she was sent down for."

"Are you saying she didn't – couldn't or wouldn't do it, and that's why she was killed?"

"That's my guess. Yes."

Stanwood reviewed the scene in the ranger shed, found it still an unbearable experience in his mind's eye. "Maybe. Dugan would have to be a pig or insane to kill her that way. You see, I was there – discovered the body."

Muldowney looked surprised. "I hadn't heard the details – how she was killed. Just the simple fact she was dead."

"Simple to you, perhaps. I'm still trying to piece it out. Another question. Why did Noreen keep coming back to Rosslare? She was through with her family and the town. Why return?"

"I suppose her roots are here. She had bad experiences up in Belfast, too. And when she was mixed up in something, on the run, perhaps she felt safer here where nobody would be looking for her."

"Working at the Strand Hotel? How safe would that be?"

"She didn't do that often. And was never here that long. Sometimes she worked for Tim Cullimore in Wexford. Waitress. She knew she was safe there. Tim has his sources, you see."

"Where did she stay? She had to sleep somewhere."

"She never told me. The same reason, you see? If somebody came looking for her, she didn't want me dragged into it. Maybe giving her away if things get too rough. Noreen knew how I was. And they could get it without having to beat it out of me. All they needed was a bottle."

"Okay, you don't know. But you've known her all her life, you say. Where would you guess she stayed?"

"Maybe at one of the caravans. It's as good as any place to hide. Nobody ever checks there. People keep moving."

"But Matt Bogson told me he owns them all. He didn't like her. Would he rent to her?"

Muldowney was downing another drink. His eyes were shining, his cheeks flushed. Truly the bottle of spirits was winning over his cold. "First, Bogson doesn't own them all. There's plenty around, all over. And second, he wouldn't have to know she was there."

"How's that?"

"Bogson doesn't do the renting. He's got a man working there. Zale. Artist chap, and good, too." He pointed to a realistic painting on the wall. "That's one of his. Noreen could have given him another name.

She pays the rent. Only Zale has the tenant listing. All Bogson is interested in is the money."

Stanwood got to his feet. "Guess I was wrong about you. I had a feeling you were in it. I can see you like a more quiet kind of life."

Muldowney grinned. "You're dead wrong on that, too. I saw you through the blinds when you first drove over. Thought you were a copper."

"What's that to you? You're clean."

"Not exactly. You see, I sell fake antiques here. Quite a bit of stolen property, too."

Stanwood stared. "How do you manage that?"

"I don't have big ideas. So I never needed an army. All I needed was a gang."

Stanwood scratched his head. "How'd you ever get started on an operation like that?"

Muldowney was tipping the bottle. He raised his glass, half full. "Noreen was the one helped me get started. She knew I wasn't too aggressive. She wanted to help me make something of myself."

"You're saying – "

"That's right. She dreamed it all up. Helped me get rich."

Stanwood shook his head. "What made her quit if you were doing so well?"

"It was too easy. Nobody caught on. She wanted more excitement out of life."

Stanwood turned to Moran. "What do you make of all that, Paddy?"

"I'm thinking it beats driving the cab. Maybe Mr. Muldowney can use a partner."

"Drop around some time. We can talk it over."

"I nearly forgot," Stanwood said. "Somebody tried to frame you for an attempted murder a while ago. Used a car to match yours. Yellow Honda. Do you have any enemies?"

"Well, I've got friends. Same thing, is it not?"

Thirty-Eight

"Now don't be thinking ill of the girl," Moran said. "This is a hard place to be for a girl with spirit."

"I'm not, Paddy. I was just thinking how different it might have been for her, if she'd left home and come over to the States like Kate did."

"Could be. But being sisters don't mean they were that much alike. And maybe this one here got herself mixed up in causes. When ye think about the wrongs in the country, you can go off a bit trying to set things to right."

They were in the Rover, moving slowly away from Muldowney's antique shop. He's right, Stanwood thought. It's all over but I still have to do my part in it. "Muldowney said he left her at the hairdresser. That was after noon on Thursday. She showed up at Rosslare the following night dressed as a witch. Maybe Cullimore can fill in what's missing. Come on, I'll buy you lunch."

"I was hoping you'd remember that, sir. A man gets thirsty once he gets started drinking in the morning."

Wexford on a Sunday morning was quiet, the tourists not yet out in force. Moran parked on Distillery Road in front of the tavern with ample parking space all around him.

The door was closed. Stanwood looked at Moran.

"It's early Sunday, sir. Times the pub owner is trying to get himself back from the night before."

Stanwood rang the bell. The door opened. Cullimore looked pale. Dark circles under puffy eyes.

"It's you, then, is it? I've been expecting you."

"This is Paddy Moran."

"Aye. McSwiney said his name. Come in, then, and I'll close the door for our talk."

"Is it too early for you to be filling a glass for me, Tim?"

Cullimore grinned. "Sit yourself down, Moran, and what do ye take me for? Me missus will be bringing in the food. Let me tell her first we've got company."

He walked to the back and called up a stairway. There was bantering talk between him and a woman's voice upstairs. He returned by way of the bar, carrying dark bottles on a tray with glasses. "Here's to you, gents," he said, starting them off. He nodded to Stanwood. "I was wrong that night, telling you to wait, sir. I knew Noreen was in trouble, but there was nought more I could tell you."

"We've just come from Muldowney's place," Stanwood said. "I've got most of the picture now. Do you have an idea who killed her?"

Cullimore stared. In the dim amber light, his rough face looked mean and haggard. "If I knew that, you wouldn't have to ask. He'd be dead himself now." He flexed his huge hands. "I didn't tell you before, and there was no need to. Noreen Kelly was like a daughter to me. And the missus. They were not that far apart in years, and Margaret, my wife, knew Noreen since she was a wee toddler."

"Does your wife come from Rosslare?"

"Aye. Used to work at the hotel. That's how Noreen got to be working there odd times. Margaret and the hotel owners, Shannons, were very close, and it didn't matter what trouble Noreen was in, they had a place for her."

"You knew about the racket she started with Muldowney?"

"Aye."

"Why didn't you stop her?"

Cullimore shrugged wide shoulders, smiling. "I was a wild one then myself. We're talking about ten years back now. She was playing her little game with Mickey, ripping off the estates, I was fighting, up North, running guns. Both of us scratching, you see, doing what we had to."

"Is that how she got started with the IRA and that stuff, following your example?"

"It wasn't only me. There were others she knew who were active. But I'm not denying it. Sure I knew the people from County Monaghan to Antrim that were fighting the British. She met some in Dublin, liked them, and got herself in. That was, what? – five years back."

An attractive dark-haired woman came in carrying a heavy tray. Cullimore rose to help her. "This is Margaret, me own darling lass. This is Mr. Paddy Moran, love, a friend of McSwiney and the gentleman here is Mr. Stanwood, who was married to Noreen's sister, you'll recall her saying."

The woman shook hands with both men. "I'll just say the one thing, Mr. Stanwood, and be off so you gentlemen can talk. Noreen was a good girl, a fine girl, no matter what you'll be hearing."

Stanwood had a sudden thought, looking at the woman. She seemed under forty, about Kate's age, and looking more closely at Cullimore now, he realized the tavern owner was nearly as old as he. "Did you know Katie?" he asked.

"Sure and I did. We grew up together in Rosslare. Kate was a year or two older, but we lived close by and were always friends." She was smiling. "Didn't she ever tell you about Maggie O'Brien?"

So many years, he'd forgotten now, of course. "She must have," he said. "It was so long ago. I remember now she would be getting letters from a friend in Ireland. Was that you?"

"Likely it was. But then after I married Tim, and she to you, soon after, the writing between us stopped. And I'm terribly sorry to hear of her dying. So young, she was. Did it go bad for her then?"

"She never let on until near the end. It must have been."

"I'll be leaving you then. Come back and see us some time."

"Did Noreen have any enemies, Mrs. Cullimore?" Her dark eyes flashed angrily. "And who would not be liking a lovely girl like her?"

Stanwood watched her go. Fine figure of a woman. Knew Noreen all the way. Same for Muldowney. Cullimore, nearly the same. Bogson and her mother are the only ones I've met who didn't like her. So who killed her? If it was the Irish assassin leader, wouldn't he have used a gun? Even a knife. It's gangland tactics we're talking about, isn't it?

"If I don't find anything down around here, Mr. Cullimore, I'll have to go up to Belfast. Could you tell me where I can find Dugan?"

"Aye. But I'll never believe Terry Dugan would kill the girl – and not that way, for a fact." He took a small book from his hip pocket, turned to a page, spreading it open before Stanwood. "The number's in my head. 21 Ben Madigan Road. You can read off the rest."

Stanwood, copying it down in his own notebook, stopped. "I've a number here – address just like it, for a Tomas Desmond, from Belfast. The girl at the Strand showed it to me."

"He just didn't use his right name, man. They're one and the same. Tomas Desmond from Belfast is Terry Dugan. You have the rest, do you? Newtown Abbey, County Antrim?"

Stanwood showed him the similar address he had
written before. Cullimore nodded assent. "I'm not
familiar how it goes in a guerrilla army, Cullimore.
How do I go about getting to see him?"

"No problem, man. You tell me where you'll be in
Dublin. Terry will be calling on you." As Stanwood
stared, he nodded. "And if he don't, I'll be breaking
his neck, for sure."

"Maybe I'll beat you to it," Stanwood said. "There's
just one question left. Last time I saw Noreen was
Thursday noon. Muldowney said he drove her to
Wexford to a beauty parlour. He says he never saw her
again. The girl in the beauty parlour never waited on
her, she told him. Noreen showed up at Rosslare the
following night. Where could she have been in the
meantime?"

Cullimore snorted. "Right here."

"Here?"

"Upstairs in our apartment. We always have a room
for her. She was safe because to get at her, they'd have
to get through me."

"When did she get here?"

"Thursday afternoon."

"Anybody in your bar see her come in?"

"She has her own key to the back door. Not likely
she was seen."

"She slept here Thursday night?"

"Aye. And had breakfast the next morning
upstairs."

"Then what?"

"She hung around most of the day, talking with
Margaret."

"What time did she leave?"

"Near dusk. About six."

"What was she wearing?" Cullimore stared, puzzled,
and he had to explain about the witch's costume.

Cullimore looked more puzzled. Stanwood continued with the antics of the Hallowe'en revellers, the witch caught in the middle, and his next sight of her, murdered in the witch's dress.

Cullimore got to his feet and walked the floor. After a few long strides back and forth, he returned to the table. "That's a puzzle, all right. Because it was I drove her to Rosslare myself. She had business there, she said, and I didn't ask what it was. But I'll tell you this. She wasn't wearing no witch's dress, like you're telling me. When she got out of the car, she was wearing her usual for this time of year. Black boots, green sweater, blouse and dark grey skirt, and a little short warm red jacket for the rain."

"Where did you drop her off?"

"Past the hotel. Near the golf course. She was going to walk around, she said."

"Any golfers still out?"

"They're daft, no doubt, but they'll not be playing in the dark."

"Where do you think she picked up the witch costume?"

"I'm thinking, man, and I cannot. Perhaps at a shop there. But no, she didn't want to be seen. There's only the one man might have done it for her."

"In Rosslare?"

"Aye. The artist man from the caravan."

"Zale, the manager?"

"Aye. He likes to dress up his models in all kinds of fancy dress. Margaret was there in his trailer for her own picture one time. The man had a regular boo-teek, she said, in there. Painted her as a queen, in proper robes. It's upstairs, if you like – "

"Maybe next time. I want to see the caravan man first."

"Tell him to come over, if he has the time. Maggie's

been after me to get one of myself done to hang next to
her own."

"Dressed like a king?"

"And why the hell not?"

Thirty-Nine

Early Sunday morning, Detectives John Shaw and
Michael Goggin had located greenkeeper Woody
Jackson setting the markers straight on the 18th tee. He
kept working while answering the questions directed at
him by the detectives, explaining that the tee markers
as they were now, would have persuaded the oncoming
tournament golfers to hit straightaway into the Irish
Sea instead of the adjacent fairway. Who would have
done a thing like turning the tee markers around? the
detectives asked. Rotten village kids, Jackson said.
They're always up to it, switching the blue women's
markers behind the men's red, and so on. On a
remembered recent complaint, Detective Goggin asked
Jackson what was wrong with the 14th green, and why
didn't it hold its shots properly, as alleged. He was told
with some asperity by the greenkeeper that anybody
voicing that complaint was probably a bad golfer, and
didn't know how to hit his irons properly high enough,
or with enough backspin to bite into the green and
hold. And then, becoming increasingly annoyed, he
asked if they had any more dumb questions as he had
work to do.

Falling into the semantic trap, Detective Goggin
asked, "Was the hut behind the 14th green where the
body was found yesterday morning usually kept
locked? The door, that is."

"No, it weren't."

"You have valuable equipment there, do you not?"

"Aye, that I do."

"And costly seeds, and mulch, and fertilizer and chemicals?"

"Aye, I do that."

"Then why did you never lock the door to the shed?"

"Because when I did, them little bastards I was telling you about, they break the lock."

"And then what do they do?"

"They kick everything about. What d'ya think?"

"Then wouldn't it make more sense to get another lock?"

"Makes sense to you two, maybe. But locks is expensive. Seeds and the other muck is cheap, and I can always shovel it back. The members will not be paying me extra money to be off buying new locks. So I put up the lock one time, to please them and do me job right. Then when it's broken off, I don't do nought. I don't sit home nights worrying about me seeds."

"Aren't you concerned that somebody got into your shed and killed a woman there?"

Jackson hammered the last blow into the marker stake and stood erect. "She was found, wasn't she?" The inquisition duo nodded. "Well, I know lots of places on this course where a body can be left lying, and chances are it'll never be found again."

Win one, lose one, was the phrase darting about in Goggin's head. *I don't know why half my life has to be spent talking to raving maniacs, or those nearly there. And when I get home, there's the missus, daft on her own from the Galway winds.* Aloud, he said, "What about the caravans, John? Might as well check out Hanna's story."

"They're right near," he said. "Well, will you look at that? There they are."

"Don't take it hard, man. He only lied every other word."

There were ten trailers inside the lot, some facing seaward, some inland, the remainder facing each other in the centre. In the event of attack by unfriendly Indians, their little stockade was well-placed.

It was still early enough Sunday morning, and nothing was stirring on the caravan grounds but the gravel under their heels. "There's the manager's office, see the sign?" Goggin said. He knocked and waited, knocked and waited. "Is he at church, do you think?"

"How would I know?" Shaw said.

A little man detached himself from the door of his trailer across the way. "You looking for the manager?"

"Yes."

"He ain't in. I knocked meself before."

"Any idea where he might be?"

"Aye. It's the end of the month, ain't it?"

Jesus, another one, Goggin thought. Why do they keep finding me? "What's the date got to do with it?"

"Plenty," said the old codger. "End of the month, Mr. Zale collects all the rent money due, and takes it over to the owner."

"Who might he be?"

"He might be anybody, but for this lot, he's Matt Bogson."

"Where's he live?"

"Cedar Burrow Lane."

"We've been there," Shaw said.

"What?" said Goggin.

"Cedar Burrow. Bogson. Mrs. Kelly. Noreen Kelly. Got it?"

"Jesus," Goggin said.

"Ask Mr. Zale to call the Wexford police when he gets back, please, sir."

"And who shall I tell him is asking, if you please?"

"The Wexford police – "

"Jesus," Goggin said.

"We never asked him the question," Shaw said. "Did he see or hear anything late Friday night?"

"So we didn't. You want to go back and ask him?"

"No."

"There's lots more where he come from. Come on."

The door to the third caravan opened a crack to Goggin's repeated knock. It was dark inside. A quavering voice said, "Yes?"

"Wexford police. Garda, ma'am. Did you see or hear anything late Friday night?"

"There was a nasty dog barking."

The door closed and Goggin said, "You take the next one."

A happy, smiling, healthy-looking woman answered Shaw's knock at the fourth caravan. There you are, Goggin thought blackly. Notice what he gets and what I draw.

"Good morning, madam. I'm sorry to interrupt you but – "

"What?"

"Wexford police, ma'am. We're investigating a crime – "

"Are you asking me the time, sir?"

"No, ma'am. It's about this past Friday night. Between the hours of ten and twelve. Did you see or hear anything unusual?" That's it, Shaw thought. Let her chew that lot over.

"I'm sorry. I'm a little hard of hearing. Would you mind repeating that?"

"Ask her how come she answered the door on the first pop," Goggin said.

"I can hear doors," the woman said. "Not people."
She stood there waiting, smiling. "Is there anything
else?"

"Not really," Shaw said.

"What?"

"That one with flowers on the sill," Goggin said.
"Right at the spot that lying bastard Hanna
mentioned. They might have the truth waiting for us.
One little knock does it. You or me?"

"Your honour. I just lost my serve."

Knock knock. "Yes?"

"Good morning, sir. Would you mind answering – "

"Yes, I would. Can't you read the sign?"

"What sign is that, sir?"

"That one there says No Soliciting."

Door slam. Heavy sigh. Officer in trouble. Jesus!

"You know something," Shaw said. "The people
here are crazy."

"Whatever gave you that idea?"

"That one there with the green curtains. Green is my
favourite colour. All my lucky days have some green in
them."

Come to think of it, he's crazy too. I've been too
busy to notice. "Would that be light green or dark,
John?"

"Don't believe me, do you? Watch."

"Yes?"

Another good looker, ooh! Blonde baby doll! Why
don't I like green?

"Garda, ma'am. Your name is – "

"Christine. And you are – ?"

"Detective John Shaw, ma'am. Wexford police."

"You're not Ralph?"

Green's as lousy as the rest of them.

"Ralph? No, ma'am. Who's Ralph?" It wouldn't be her husband now, would it? She'd know him on sight, would she not?

"I'm expecting a Ralph. My astrologer said Sunday morning a stranger by the name of Ralph would come into my life."

Ralph, it's a name I always liked, Goggin thought bitterly. But what did they give me? Michael. Low on the list with these astrologers. "Forget it, Johnny," he said. "We'll find you another pretty colour."

"What's *your* name?" the woman asked Goggin.

"Sorry, madam," he said. "We are not allowed to give out that information."

"That's silly. He gave his."

She was such a stunner, Shaw decided to be charitable and make the moment last. "He's not allowed to give his name unless you prove to be a reliable witness."

She had gorgeous eyes, and Ralph didn't know what he was missing. "Witness to what?"

"Late Friday night. About ten. Somebody got knocked over the head in the lot here. Did you happen to – "

"That must have been Ralph. Somebody here is jealous of me."

"You said Sunday morning, according to your astrologer."

"Well, they don't know it all, do they? Friday night is close enough for a stranger."

"Come on, Johnny."

"Then I take it you didn't hear or see anything Friday night?"

"Well, not here, anyway. I was up in a Dublin hotel with my astrologer."

"Oh? Well, thank you very much. Those are lovely green curtains you have."

"Oh, are they green? I'm colour blind, you see."

So it went. Luck was not with them on this lovely Sunday morning, with the sun shining, the air pure and bracing, and little Noreen Kelly found dead at a murderer's hand only the day before.

They were at the Strand Hotel taking down the names of all out-of-town guests when word reached them of the shooting down of the British golfer after an excellent tee shot, and requiring only a moderate 8-iron to the pin. Almost a certain birdie on the 11th hole, a long 478-yard par 5, and perhaps an eagle. The yellow car speeding from the scene had been critically observed by various keen-eyed onlookers as a Honda, Toyota Corolla and Citroen.

There were eye-witnesses who knew for certain that Mickey Muldowney of Ennisworthy drove a small yellow Honda. Inasmuch as he was next on their interrogative list anyway because of George Hanna's testimony, they called their station in Wexford to ascertain Muldowney's address. In doing so, they learned of another Honda being impounded under protest by a Wexford dealer named Travis Mac-Mcnamin, and a tin barrel of debris collected from Kilmore's Kar Wash.

"What's that all about?" Goggin wondered out loud.

Shaw who had seen better days responded with unexpected savagery. "If you'll step harder on the pedal, we'll soon find out."

Cracking up, he is, thought Goggin, and for what? It's only a job. Since Shaw was his superior, however, by virtue of longer tenure of approximately two weeks, Goggin did not argue and put his big foot down in a spasmodic reflex. They were squirting down the highway from Rosslare to Wexford and vice-versa when a large, old Rover coming from the opposite direction, its driver keeping his left wheel by cabbie's divine right centred squarely on the highway dividing line, forced Goggin over. As it passed, Goggin cursed all drivers of big cars, and then suddenly observed: "Hey, did you notice who was in there? That was Stanwood, the bloody Yank."

"Keep your mind on the driving," Shaw said curtly. "You bloody near got us sideswiped."

Nevertheless Goggin could not centre his mind completely, and a small part of it raised a nagging, familiar question. Wonder what that's all about?

Forty

Stanwood stepped out of the Rover at the caravan site and stuck his hand out. "Thanks, Paddy, and I don't think I'll be seeing you again. Not this trip. Do I owe you any money?"

"Not at all, sir. You've not had any luck then, with it?"

"As a matter of fact, it's gone better than I'd thought. Just a few more bits to put together, and I'm done here."

"You know who did the deed then?"

"Oh, yes. I think so. I'm still hunting for the reason."

"Well, goodbye, then, and God keep you."

The Rover turned around, and he walked into the caravan site. He was approaching the trailer with the sign MANAGER on it, when hailed from across the path.

"He's not in."

"Who's not in?"

"You're looking for Mr. Zale, the manager, are you not?"

"If he's the one who rents the trailers. Who are you?"

"Regis Bundy. I'm in that one there. You looking for month-to-month or permanent quarters?"

"It all depends. When will Mr. Zale be back?"

"No telling. Went over to deliver the rent money to Mr. Bogson earlier, I'm thinking, and he's not been back. A couple of other men were asking for him this morning, earlier on."

"Mind if I look around?"

"I can tell you all you want to know. I been here the longest. Except for that end one there at the back. Number 8. Mrs. Gantry. She was here before me." He began to cackle to himself. "She's been here the longest, but also been here the least."

"What does that mean?"

"It means she's hardly ever around. Nobody ever sees her. Oh, I've seen her, at times. But not to speak to. Big flashy redheaded woman, she is. With airs like she's just left the Prime Minister. Got her own town house in Dublin, I understand. Another woman staying with her this time, I noticed."

"Well, that's all right, isn't it? It's like your own home or apartment once you get it, isn't it?"

"Aye. Come to think of it, I'm the only one who's at all friendly here. Nobody in the lot talks much."

Stanwood was familiar with the type of people who live in cheap hotels or rundown surroundings for their own reasons. "If I want one of these, what's it cost?"

"There's none vacant now, so it'll do you no good to ask. There're others, you know. Toward Wexford they got the municipal caravan and camping site there. That'd be cheapest."

Stanwood thought about it. "I'd like to speak to the manager anyway. Maybe something might turn up soon. For a couple of pounds, do you think you might go up and fetch him?"

He was peeling paper notes from his roll. The man snatched at them. He cackled hoarsely. "Aye, the five will do me fine." Man's a fool with his money, he thought. "Now it'd be a long walk up to Cedar Burrow where he's gone to, if you don't mind the wait."

"I'm in no hurry. Take your time, Mr. Bundy."

He watched Bundy trundle off with his walking stick. The site was quiet. No sounds of children at play. No loud voices raised in connubial disharmony. Somewhere a radio played softly as he neared Zale's hut. He looked again at Number 8 facing the sea. It was like the rest. Painted white. Nothing fancy. Curtains and drawn blinds. If the woman owned an elegant town house, down here was where she could let her hair down. Be like ordinary folks.

He mounted the step and knocked on the manager's door. There was no answer. He turned the knob. The door was unlocked and he walked in. On such simple procedures do great detectives operate.

The caravan with blinds drawn was dark. Stanwood stopped, scenting like an animal. He knew before he found the light. The smell of blood told him murder had been done.

Lying face down amid a clutter of his sketches and paintings, Donald Zale had accomplished something in the nature of a paradox. In a lifetime devoted to the perfection of his art, he had found it only in the artful manner of his death. The long-bladed kitchen knife sunk nearly to the hilt below his left shoulder blade, had found the aortic artery with such unerring despatch that he hardly bled outwardly.

He touched the man's throat with the back of his

hand, and estimated death as having occurred late the previous night. The body was cold, in rigor. Midnight, perhaps? Within an hour or two. As the pathologists note it. And who are we to question Stanwood's guess? The man had been finding bodies warm, luke-warm and cold more than half his life. Take his word for it.

An open metal money box was near his cold hand. Tenant cheques, no cash. All made out to Bogson Caravans. He counted nine. Equal to the number of caravans rentable with the manager living there free. Noreen Kelly hadn't signed any. A small book listed accounts and tenant names. He pocketed it.

Moving quickly, he went through the dwelling. Small kitchen, toilet and shower stall, living room, front parlour turned into a studio, curtained off from the rest. Cullimore's wife Margaret had told him true. There were goods enough for any boutique. On racks, chests, overflowing drawers and small tables. A motley collection of costumes, period dresses, cheap costume jewellery, shoes, slippers, wigs and bonnets. Used by his models, not for sale.

He lifted the lid of a small wicker chest. The black boots were missing, but the rest was there. Green sweater, blouse, grey skirt, pile-lined red hip-hugging storm jacket. Underneath, the other missing item he had been searching for. Shoulder bag. Purse inside. Stuff girls carry. Cosmetics, mirror, comb. Address book. Notes.

Given to talking to himself of late, as well as others less fortunate, he said softly, "Well, Noreen, now at last we know where you transformed yourself into the witch."

He wondered why, and how, she had got herself trapped inside the circle of Rosslare children celebrating Hallowe'en. Why did she run from the beauty shop? Why come here? Questions came easier than answers. He went back to Zale's still body. Something gleamed under his hip. He found a ring of numbered keys clipped to Zale's belt. He slipped off one, numbered 8. Was she the one driving the phantom Honda? Occupied or not, he had to get inside there.

He returned to studying Zale's work. Managing the caravans had still allowed him time for producing hundreds of pictures. They were in pencil, ink or colour, some rough quick sketches, others in fine detail, preliminaries for finished works. Stanwood recalled the excellent landscape on the Strand Hotel wall. Apparently he was compulsively impelled to sketch anything he saw.

Stanwood recognized a sketch of the old man at number 2 across the way, Bundy. There was a mean caricature of Bogson, piglike and lifelike. Mrs. Kelly leaned against a tree, standing with a sweet smile for the artist. Many drawings were small, letter size, off a pad. Some posed. Some drawn, caught offguard. One of Doyle, the headwaiter. Sheila Nolan, the blonde desk girl there. Muldowney. Mary Garner on the beach. Lovely figure. Some had names scrawled at the bottom, faces he didn't recognize. Molly Packer. George Hanna. Mrs. Shannon. Albert Rattigan. Kilty with a rubbery golf club. Golfers on the links. Hunters.

There was one in colour Stanwood could not resist stealing. Noreen, with her long hair flaming red, the brilliant blue eyes. Zale was good. He rooted around now for something of the mysterious big, flashy redhead. The longtime part-time tenant of number 8. Mrs. Gantry, according to Bundy. There was nothing. Elusive even to Zale, he thought. He returned to the costume section, studied the wigs, a red one particularly, and then walked out.

Forty-One

The manager's tenant book listed the occupant of No. 8 as Maureen Gantry. An address in Cornwall. One in Dublin, Lansdowne Rd. Ballsbridge.

He was halfway there. He noticed green curtains move inside a caravan on his left. A door opened. A very attractive blonde woman stood swaying, showing a warm inviting smile. "Are you Ralph?" she asked.

"No, ma'am. Sorry."

"Oh, too bad."

The door closed. No mystery about that one, he thought. He skirted the other caravans. The car park area was to the far side. He saw a small tan Toyota, a yellow Fiat, a small yellow Austin. Don't tell me, he told himself. I'll hate myself.

The tyres were warm, also the radiator and hood. Well, why not? It's a warm day. There was gravel in the tyre treads. Gravel, too, in the driveway. The turning-about area was gravel, with dirt and grass. Let's check inside first before we start collecting another pocketful.

Why put her body in the golf shed? he asked himself, on another tangent. What did that gain? It was sure to be found. Or was that the idea?

He walked around number 8. The rear door opened to the beach beyond. The blinds were down and he heard no sound. He tapped lightly at the door. No response. He tried the doorknob. It was locked. So it goes.

The key from the manager's cluster fitted, and he stepped inside. There was an overpowering feminine scent and Stanwood's first thought was that he had walked into a whorehouse. He walked around, amending his thought. Well, call it a pleasure palace for a happy hedonist.

Lush was the word. Thick burgundy carpeting. Frilly drapes. Crimson walls in the bedroom dotted with soft aquatint etchings. Expensive perfumes littered the white vanity table. There were mirrors everywhere, and he looked instinctively at the ceiling, saw no glass reflection and murmured, "Landlord refused permission?"

The closet was filled with expensive clothes. Labels from Paris, Dublin, London. Soft robes and nightdresses. Gold (why not) open-toed slippers. Hats and hat boxes. Capes and furs. The dresser drawers had a plethora of all the intimate garments known to man (some) and women (nearly all).

Probing in the bottom drawer he found pictures and a blonde wig. The pictures were of men, looking happy and refreshed. Well, reasonably so. He tried the wig on. Did he look like a big flashy broad? He smiled in the mirror. Terrible sight, that. More like a big fat ex-cop.

There was food in the fridge. Cold beer, wine. Butter and cream were fresh. Mrs. Gantry had made a recent appearance. He sniffed at the range. Burned something? Perhaps quite recently. He'd better collect what he must and get out.

He went back to the drawer with the pictures. There was one he had missed, tucked in a folder. Tall chap with thick wavy hair. His arm around a slim girl. They both looked happy. The girl looked like Noreen Kelly.

He studied the man's face. It looked familiar but he didn't make the connection until he recalled a small sketch the late artist-manager had made. George Hanna?

Who took the photo? Don't ask me. What was Noreen doing with that chap? If I knew all the answers I wouldn't still be here looking.

He counted an even dozen of men's photos, all on holiday from their attire. Some young, some older. What difference does it really make when you're bent on pleasure?

He took the photo of Hanna and Noreen along with the blonde wig as keepsakes, and departed as he had come, unseen. If you don't count Christine.

Forty-Two

Back in his hotel room, Stanwood called Tim Cullimore.

"What can I do for you, lad?"

"I found Noreen's clothes at Bogson's caravan site. The manager Zale's pad. He had all kinds of costumes there, as your wife said. Apparently he had one for a witch, too, and loaned it to her."

"Did he tell you why?"

"He couldn't. Somebody killed him before I got there."

"You think it's the same person who did in Noreen?"

"It's possible. Noreen's handbag was there. An address book. Some notes. I can leave it at the hotel desk for you."

"I'm much obliged. Are you leaving then?"

"Next stop Dublin, maybe Belfast. How will I find Dugan?"

"Call me when you find your hotel. He'll be calling you."

"One more thing, Tim. Are you familiar with the name Hanna?"

"Sounds like a chap Noreen knew. They had a little romance going at one time."

"George Hanna?"

"That's the name. Chap from Galway. Married, with a couple of kids. Details like that can spoil a romance."

"Noreen never told you why she was going back to Rosslare that Friday night?"

"No, and I didn't ask. I stay out of it now. I've Maggie to think about."

"Is it possible she had an assignment from her group – to knock off somebody – one of the visiting VIP golfers?"

"Sure it's possible. It don't mean she'd have done it."

"She ran from the hair stylist shop. Can you think of any reason?"

"I've been trying to, since you left. Nothing."

"Did she get any telephone calls at your place?"

"None I know of. Hold on, I'll ask Margaret." He was off the line for a few moments. "She says she told me and I forgot. Some chap called. Left a message for Noreen who was out. Said it was urgent she meet him the usual place at ten."

"Did you give Noreen the message?"

"No, I guess Margaret did." A voice shouted from the distance that indeed she had.

"Any idea who it was? Any name?"

"Did the man give a name, love?" There was more yelling back and forth. "No, he didn't."

"It could be Dugan or Hanna."

"Listen, man. It could be anybody."

Stanwood thought about it. "You've got a point there."

Forty-Three

He was downstairs at the reception desk with his bag.

"Bill Stanwood, don't tell me you're leaving!"

It was strange that she looked more beautiful each time he saw her. "There's just time for me to catch the next train to Dublin. I was going to leave a note for you."

"Oh, this is terrible! We've hardly had time to know each other. Must you go?"

"I've found the answer isn't here. Maybe I'll find it up there." Somehow he was holding her hand, sounding apologetic, feeling terrible. "You know how compulsive I am on these matters. I guess I'll always be a copper."

"I know. Oh, darn!" A new thought made her eyes dance and her radiant smile return. "But after that, after you've done your business, or whatever it is you do, you don't have to go right back to the States, do you?"

"No. I thought I'd made it clear. There's nothing there for me now – "

She had her bag open. "Well, then why don't you visit me in Wales? It's just across on a ferry ride. Here's my card. And wait – I'll write my home phone number."

He studied the card, frowning. "Is that an address? All those consonants together? Don't your people know about vowels?"

She laughed. "I know lots much worse. That is Bryn-Newydd. In Prestatyn. The last word is C-l-w-y-d. It's in North Wales."

He put the card in his pocket. "I'd very much like to see you again. No question about it. See how you work your school for those kids. But now this has come up. Any idea when you'll be back there?"

Her eyes moistened. "Well, there's not much to hold me here now, either. I thought … well, very likely in a few days. Now you're giving me your word, aren't you? You will call?"

"I'll do better. I promise I'll be seeing you." I've waited this long, he thought, and I can wait a bit longer.

Sheila came out from behind the reception desk. "Come along now, Mr. Stanwood. I'll be driving you to the station so you'll not be missing your train."

He groaned. "That little car of yours?"

"It's all right, sir. You can use part of my side."

Forty-Four

He found the shop on Dawson Street in Dublin just across from the Hibernian Hotel. Hairgoods International, the sign said. Just like the little label he had found tucked under a knot inside the wig. With its Dublin address.

How does one go about tracing an errant wig? There are ways. Pay attention.

"It's an awkward problem," Stanwood was telling the elegant male clerk. He took a ten-pound note from his pocket and placed it on the counter. "And I'd like to pay you for your trouble."

The clerk's hand gobbled up the note. No problem that can't be solved for a tenner, Jack. "No trouble at all, sir. What is it?"

Stanwood placed the blonde wig on the counter. "First, is this one of yours?"

The man turned it over, saw his own house label, and nodded. Stupid ass, what does it say there? "Yes, sir, it is."

"Good. Well, what I'd like to know is whose it is."

The clerk stared, puzzled. What'd he do, find it in the john? "I beg your pardon, sir?"

"It's like this," Stanwood said. "My wife and I were just down at this hotel in Rosslare. And she and another lady were using the pool. Then they went in to have their hair done – the hotel hairdresser, their own shop there. And I don't understand it but somehow the wigs got mixed up. My wife's and this other lady's. So if you could trace it, we'd be ever so grateful."

Sure you would. Prove it with another tenner, sport. "One moment, sir. I'll have to check that serial number on the back with our records."

He returned quickly with a box of file cards and a ledger. He opened the ledger. "There you are, sir. No problem."

Stanwood was copying down the name and address listed. "You're positive this is the correct name and address of the owner of this wig? No chance of error?"

"Not likely, sir, considering that we have made to order, in addition, one red and one brunette wig for the same customer. We'd be happy to return it for you, sir."

"Well, thank you, but we can't do that yet. You see, this party has my wife's wig now. And we have to try to work it out, you see, first."

"I see, sir. Something like an exchange of hostages."

"That's it. Well, I'm much obliged."

That's a crock. She probably left it in his bed thinking that was the last of him, and now he wants another crack at it. "Not at all, sir. My pleasure, indeed."

Forty-Five

The call came to his room later. "You Stanwood?"

"Yes."

"Tim tells me you want to have a talk."

"That's right."

"Know where St. Stephen's Green is? It's just up the street from you."

"Where? It's a big park."

"Easy, Jack. I've got it worked. There's an entrance on Grafton Street. Off Baggott. You walk left, turn right at the circle. Across on your left is a bench. A man will be sitting there reading a newspaper."

"In the rain?"

"All right. He'll have it on his knee. You come over and ask if you can have a look at the paper. If he doesn't belt you then, you found my man. He gives you the paper and goes. You sit down there with it. Got it?"

"When does all this happen?"

"He's out there now getting his bloody head wet."

The street was alive with black bobbing umbrellas. Excepting the space over Stanwood. He hated the contraptions, had never used one. He simply accepted getting soaked with the privilege then of bitching about it.

The park was confined within long iron palings. Was someone going to steal it? The outer path was deserted. Inside the large circular opening were cobblestones, flowers, an overflowing fountain, benches. A wet man sat on one, soggy newspaper over one knee. No imagination there. He could have used the financial section to cover his head.

Stanwood had played silly games before. "Mind if I

borrow your paper?"

The man stood up. Seamed irregular face. Long jaw and blue searching eyes. Wet bent cigarette on his lip. Handing him the soggy lump. "There you are, mate. They'll be along soon."

There were three of them, moments later. The broad-shouldered man in the middle the only one civil enough to speak. "You were told to be sitting there with it. Not on your bloody feet."

"Up yours, Dugan. I'm here for a talk, not pneumonia."

"Well, then. Walk ahead down this path. There'll be a black car at the end opening. Get in the back seat and don't look behind."

More games. Well, the man was wanted, no doubt, for this and that. Good fellow, too. Didn't care for umbrellas, either.

The walk was short, uneventful. Long-stemmed flowers lined the path. One of these days, he thought, I'm going to be able to tell which is which. Stupid not knowing.

The long black car was there, roomy enough to take them all. Dugan flanked him on his right. Another man stepped in on his left. The third sat next to the driver.

"We'll be going to a pub to talk. Not far."

The car was powerful and knew its way. Left on Haddington Road, right on Umberland, past the River Liffey, left on a short street, even through an alley toward Irishtown and Dublin Bay. Cigarette smoke did all the conversation.

The pub was near the waterfront behind the station. He heard a train clacking not far off. "We'll go in together like old friends. There's a room in the back. Had your lunch yet? Good. Foley makes the best meat pie in all Dublin."

"McSwiney's wife does a damn good one."

Dugan roared. "The little pub in Wexford town? Damn, but you're right. Come to think of it, hers is got Foley's beat."

The outer room was full of men, smoke and loud talk. Dugan's man led the way straight through. Stanwood noticed the quick-averting eyes of the men standing around the bar. VIP here, you don't know nothing, so you can't say nothing.

There were three tables, bare walls, an eerie overhead light. Stanwood followed Dugan to the table near the far wall. His men sat close to the front, beside the door.

"So you know Tim Cullimore, do you not?"

"I'm here to talk about Noreen Kelly, not him."

"Aye. You're the copper was married to Kate." His grey eyes squinted at Stanwood through the cigarette smoke. "Met the family, did you?"

There was a short buzzing sound in the room. Dugan nodded. His man tapped on the door and it opened. A shirt-sleeved man with an open green worn vest stood there. "What'll you be having?" His eyes skipped Stanwood.

"Bring us your pies, Foley, and the glasses to go along with it." To Stanwood, he said, "You like the bitter brown or the beer?"

"Beer is fine."

"Off you go, Foley. And how goes it with Eileen?"

"Still got the wee cough, but the fever is gone."

"Give her my best, man."

Stanwood had the picture out of his pocket before the pub owner had closed the door. "Do you know this man with Noreen?"

Dugan held it close. *Christ, the man is near-sighted. It's a wonder he saw me in the park.* "Now that's a damn fine picture of the lass."

Stanwood looked close to having a tantrum. "Look, Dugan. I don't know how many guns you have in this room. But if you don't answer my questions, I'll kill you right here."

Dugan smiled. "Aye, and if you're not the one, me Uncle Tim is waiting to be next."

"Cullimore's your uncle?"

"Aye, and that's why I'll answer you. Now you look strong enough to do what you say, but knowing Tim, he's the one to fear."

"Okay. What about the picture?"

"That's a man she's known a long time. George Hanna."

"What do you know about him?"

"There's not that much. He's a man from Galway. Married with some young ones. Comes to Rosslare to play golf. Sometimes to see Noreen."

"You don't think he killed her?"

"No more than I."

"Maybe. Was Noreen down there to do a hit job for your outfit?"

Thick brows raised. Grey eyes looked amused. "What gives you that idea?"

"Stop horsing around, Dugan. Was she on a job for you?"

"A man was hit. How can I answer you?"

"Sunday morning. She was killed on Friday night. Were you at the hotel then?"

"Aye. Waiting to speak to Noreen. I wanted to tell her she didn't have to go through with it. It wasn't needed. We'd find something else she could do and be comfortable with."

"Did you call her at your uncle's? Leave a message for her to meet you later Friday night? Usual place?"

"Not I. Who told you that?"

"Your uncle. Maggie gave him the message. She was

scared out of the beauty parlour in Wexford. Know anything about that?"

"Nought. Neither that nor the message. Who was it calling, a man?"

"So Tim said. According to his missus."

The lank Irish guerrilla leader was still studying the small photo. "Did you show this picture to Mickey Muldowney?"

"No, why?"

"I'm wondering who it was took it."

"So am I."

"It was taken a year ago. I can tell you that much."

"How do you know?"

"That little blouse Noreen is wearing. I bought it for her here in Dublin. For her birthday, it was."

"Was she Hanna's girl or yours?"

"I'll allow you the liberty, seeing as how you're in the family. George knew her first. She was my girl at the end."

"Then you didn't kill her?"

"Will you listen to the man! I want to know more than you do."

"You checked out of the hotel late Friday. Where did you go next?"

"I had a job to do, and was needed up here."

"Then you never got the chance to tell Noreen she didn't have to do the job, murder somebody that was a stranger to her?"

Dugan spread his big hands. "This is your first trip to Ireland. You'll never begin to understand the reasons for what we do. Some living here don't understand it themselves. It's a war we see in different ways. But as I said, it wasn't in Noreen to pull the trigger."

"Anybody else down there from your party that might have killed her, knowing she wouldn't go through with it?"

"Not to my knowledge. If they did, they'd know they'd be in the ground themselves now."

"Do you know a man called Zale? Donald Zale?"

"Aye, the artist bloke. Very talented man, he is."

"He was killed late Saturday night, or early Sunday morning."

"Was he now? Where was the body found?"

"In his own caravan on the lot. I found it there. I'm the one who found Noreen, too, you know, in the golf course shed."

"Did you figure out yet why she was put there?"

"Not yet. That's why I'm here to ask you the questions."

"Aye. And where was this picture found? Was it in there along with Donnie Zale?"

"Why would it be in Zale's place?"

"Well, the man was some kind of a peeper, was he not? He was always at it, drawing everything he laid his eyes on. A compulsion it was, with the man."

"I had the same impression looking through his work. An awful lot of it. But Zale would have drawn these two, wouldn't he? Why snap them with a camera?"

"Aye, you've a point. Then where was it found?"

"I can't tell you that yet, Mr. Dugan. Your temper's as bad as mine. When I get to the bottom of this, with no mistake, I'll let you know."

"Fair enough."

"What do you know about Matt Bogson?"

"That swine? I had to knock him down one time."

"Funny. I wanted to, but held back. I was in their house."

"Mouthing off about Noreen, was he not?"

"Among other things, yes."

"You'll be guessing the reason. The old pig fancied her hisself, he did. And Noreen made it only worse laughing at the sod."

"How long ago did you hit him?"

Dugan looked at his knuckles. They remembered. "Month or two back. I was down there looking for a place for her to stay. He had a vacancy on his lot. The girl would have been safe there, I thought, for the odd time when she had to hide."

"So he turned you down."

Dugan laughed shortly. "Not a bit. That's when I found out he wanted her. Thought she'd be easy pickings for him out there all alone. So I straightened him out on that score."

"Is he left-handed? Noreen was killed with a left-handed blow."

"What's it matter? Bogson's strong as an ox. Could kill a man with either hand."

"You think he might have done it?"

"Till now, I haven't heard better."

"There's the old lady, too. She hated Kate and she hated Noreen. Maybe she found out the old man wanted her youngest."

"Aye. Mrs. Kelly might have. But it's not her style with the golf club. She'd have used her own kitchen knife."

"Well, there was one sticking out of Zale's back. But it was driven too deep. I doubt she had the power for that one."

"She's old, yes, but not that weak a woman."

"Is she paralyzed?"

Dugan stared. "What give you that idea?" Stanwood explained and Dugan shook his head, his eyes dancing. "Just an act. The old bitch can walk good as you or I when she wants to."

"That's very interesting. I'm done now. Thanks for meeting me. I wish to hell you'd get out of what you're doing, and find something else."

"It's too late now, man. Noreen is dead. We were to be married soon."

"Oh, Jesus!"

"You had the same, and you know. What's it matter now?"

He was patting the man's hand. Two big murderous hands, both aquiver with sentiment. "I'm sorry, Terry. Yeah, I know."

"Will you be wanting another beer?"

"No. How do I get out of here to where I want to go?"

"Where are you going?"

"Dublin Castle. To see the Chief Superintendent of the Irish Detective Branch."

Dugan pushed his chair back. "Come on, then. We'll drive you there."

Forty-Six

"There's your brother waiting outside in my office. He'd like a few words with you."

Chief Superintendent Gallagher leaned back in his chair. "What the hell's the matter with you, Amos? You know I don't have any brother."

"I know that, sir. Will you see him? Says his name is William Stanwood."

Gallagher roared. "The Yank? What's he doing up here? Show him in, Amos. My word. Stanwood."

He was on his feet in a moment, staring and grinning. So was Stanwood. The resemblance was uncanny. Both big men, with the same solid cast to their faces, they could have been twins.

"I'll be damned," Gallagher said. "Is it me or you there?"

Moore was so delighted, he had no time for inner carping. "Do you want me to stay, sir?"

"By all means, Amos. I'm too stunned to ask the proper questions. By all means. Jesus, but I'm glad to see you looking like the man I thought you were."

There he goes, Moore thought. At it again. Oh, well, this time I'll not begrudge the man his failings.

They found Stanwood a comfortable chair. Moore found the glasses and the bottle. They found themselves drinking, smoking and laughing. Acting like kids in Dublin Castle.

"Well, what have you been up to lately?"

"I just had lunch with an interesting man."

"Who might that be?"

"Terry Dugan."

Gallagher nearly choked on his drink. "You see, Amos? Didn't I tell you?" Before Moore could think of the proper retort, Gallagher said, "You ought to be more careful while you're here, Mr. Stanwood. Dugan's a wanted, dangerous man. You might have been shot down along with him."

"I suppose. But he drove me to the door and went off okay, so all's well."

"Dugan did that? Right to the door of Dublin Castle, did he? Do you hear, Amos?"

Aye, and I'm not that deaf. "Have you, uh – reached any conclusions about the, uh – matter down in Rosslare, Mr. Stanwood? It's our understanding there's been another murder."

"Yes. I found Zale's body Sunday afternoon. That threw me off some, but then one thing led to another, and now it's over. That's why I'm here."

"You've found the murderer?"

"Let's say I've an idea who it is. It's your country. I'll

leave it up to you to decide how to wrap it up."

"That's decent of you. Any word from the two of them down in Rosslare, Amos?"

"Negative, sir. They're going through the caravan site. Taking prints. Checking out the tenants. Possible witnesses. The usual routine, sir."

Gallagher stood up and walked about. "True, it's up to us. I'd just like to hear your views on the matter."

"Well, I'd like to leave the evidence with you. I've enough now but you might want more. Then, with your permission, I'd like to see the killer face to face. That's all. You see, I still don't have the reason. Maybe I'll get it now."

"You're sure of your man?"

"Reasonably sure. Then again, it might still blow up in my face. I've had that experience before."

"What do you think, Amos? Do we give Stanwood his head?"

Oh, no, you're not dumping this on me. No way. "It's up to you, sir. After all, you run the department." As if he didn't know. Anyway, what can I do or say? Now I got two of them to deal with, same mentality. "Let's hear it all, anyway."

Stanwood emptied his pockets. "Donald Zale, first. The clippings in this envelope, the dirt, gravel and grass came off a car newly washed. Your technical men should be able to match it up with the site off the Rosslare Golf Club from which one of the visiting golfers was shot. Witnesses there saw the car pull out after the shot. I tracked it down to Wexford, The Honda car is impounded, and they'll be checking it for prints. It was all a diversion to frame Michael Muldowney."

Prints, Moore thought. The old man won't like that stuff.

Gallagher was rocked, no question about it. "What's this to do with the Zale murder?"

"The car dealer in Wexford, Travis MacMenamin, gave me a description of the person who had taken the Honda out overnight on a trial run basis. The car-wash owner, Kilmore, had a similar description. Big, flashy redheaded woman with a come-on smile.

"I found this wig at her place. Caravan 8 on the Bogson site in Rosslare." They were staring. "Mrs. Maureen Gantry."

"This one's blonde. You said red – "

"You'll find the red one in Zale's place. Both were made at the same shop on Dawson Street here in Dublin. The clerk traced it for me. Made to order. Here's the name and address he gave me."

"That's not the same name you just gave us."

"No, sir. But it's also the name of the person who killed Noreen Kelly."

What's he doing? Moore thought. Calling this evidence? "You've got more proof somewhere, perhaps?"

"Here's a photo found in hut number 8. That's Noreen with an old friend, perhaps lover, George Hanna."

"Hm, yes. The chap from Galway. Lost his mashie, did he not?"

"Detectives Shaw and Goggin released him, sir."

"Your lab men can have the colour photo traced to the lab processing it. And they in turn will give you the name of the person turning in the film. It should be Mrs. Gantry."

"Well, yes, Stanwood, but still – "

"There are stains on the kitchen floor of number 8. Similar stains on a pair of sneakers in the woman's closet. Your forensic people should be able to match those up with the fungicides in the greenkeeper's shed where the body was placed. There will be additional evidence in darker blood stains, I'm sure, mixed with the kinds of seeds and fertilizer used on that course. Some of it had spilled out, you see."

"Well, yes, we've a damn good technical staff here, but – "

"In Zale's hut, or rather studio, you'll find hundreds of drawings. Thousands, perhaps. He drew everything and everybody he saw. You'll find sketches of them all there. Residents of Rosslare and the hotel staff, visitors, accurate drawings of everybody. Or I should say, nearly everybody."

"Well, I suppose we'll find your Mrs. Gantry there and – "

"No, sir. That's what clinched it, you see. She was the only one missing. She'd rented that caravan for years. Zale had the front one for years. It was impossible, even given her rare visits, that the compulsive sketch artist would have missed drawing her."

"You're certain? Checked them all?"

"Yes, sir."

"Rare visitor, you said. What the hell does that mean? She rented that number 8 one, you told us."

"A home away from home, Mr. Gallagher. Used it to kick over the traces, you might say. Her real home address is on that slip of paper I gave you. Correct name, too."

"Hm. Going by act of omission, then, are you?"

"Why not? It makes sense."

"I like it. By God, I like it. What do you think, Amos?"

Well, Christ, if you like it, I better like it, too. "It seems a well-taken point, sir."

"Your assumption is, then, the woman, the killer, visited Zale's cottage, his caravan, killed him and took away any sketch he might have made of her, to remove any trace of her. Why'd she have to kill him? She could have burgled her way inside when he was out, found her pictures, and gone off with them."

"Yes, but as long as Zale was alive, he would still be able to identify her. Draw her from memory."

"Hm. Amos?"

I'll pass this one. "Did you tell us yet how and why this mystery woman Gantry killed Noreen Kelly?"

"No. I'm still working on that. I'm just leaving all this here in the event something goes wrong. And you'll still be able to close it out and get your conviction."

"You can have one of our men along, if you like."

"No thanks. This is a personal matter, you see."

"Well, good luck, Stanwood. Come back and see us again when it's all over."

"Sure thing. If I can."

Forty-Seven

Her voice was as he remembered it, cultivated and warm, and now over the phone intriguingly close. "What a delightful surprise! Where are you, Bill?"

"I'm at – no, damned if I can pronounce it. But the man here says it's a short ride – about twenty minutes."

"Wonderful! You'll still be in time to see the children before school closes. Stay on the left when the main road branches off. It's the first right turn after the golf course. You'll see the big white sign."

"Is it a large school? Where'll I find you?"

"Rather small, by your standards, and I'll be in my office. Just ask the matron."

The ride out was picturesque. Rolling hills with glimpses of the sea past rugged cliffs. He passed the sign Prestatyn Golf Club outside Bryn-Newydd, and thought bleakly of how he would manage things after this visit. She knows me better than I know her, he thought. She'll understand why I have to see it through.

The grounds were undulating, spacious, the long winding gravel path at the gate bordered by giant oaks and cedars. It stood gleaming white at the crest of a hill, like a jewel, a 2-storey Georgian fretted by rows of tall windows. It should be on a postcard, Stanwood thought. Some early lord's estate.

Cars were parked in the large circular driveway. He heard happy screaming voices of children at play. There was a tennis court, croquet markers, roped swings hanging from trees, and beyond the school building, below the dipping incline, boats resting with littls sails, a deep blue lake framed by tall dark pines.

The matron sat outside the door reading. He gave his name. "This way, please. Miss Garner is expecting you."

The corridor was dark with wood-panelling, high ceiling. Highly polished doors along the way were closed. He heard children singing, encouraged by a piano, a soft-voiced teacher, stopping their chant with a tapping stick, resuming a few more bars and pausing again for her modulated instructions. Wonderful, he thought. They sound great.

Her office was bright, almost masculine in the severity of its décor. Sturdy lamps on thick high bases. Dark, heavy drapes. Bookcases lined from floor to ceiling. Wide, neatly arranged desk.

"Bill! How wonderful to see you! Did you get lost on the way?"

"No. I followed all the signs I couldn't pronounce."

"I can show you places in Wales where you'd spend a day just trying to read *one*."

She was standing close, both hands on his, her always-ready smile as mischievous as the tea-coloured eyes. "No, thanks," he said. "I'll take your word for it." Well, there you are, he told himself, you'll never be able to say what's in your heart, and you might as well be dead, man.

"Care to see the grounds? We have our own little lake, you know. Too cold for swimming now but we've a few small boats the children are crazy about."

"I noticed. I was expecting a little dumpy place."

"We had that once. But children expand with more space. Freeing their bodies has a marvellous effect on freeing their minds, too."

He followed her out of a side door. "You've got the right idea."

"How did it go on your trip? Did you find what your compulsive mind was driving you to? You had some bits to clear up, you said."

"It helped, I'll say that. Not everything yet. But I'm getting there. Anything happen after I left Rosslare?"

She gripped his arm tighter. "I nearly forgot. There was another murder. Some man down in those – what are they called – the little caravans. Created quite a fuss."

"Not bad for a peaceful little place. Two murders in less than a week."

"Wait! There was a shooting, too. One of the golfers was shot. Were you there then?"

"I knew something had happened. I was out on the course, saw the commotion."

"Someone might have thought you'd done it. Leaving so soon afterward. I, at least, had the prudence to stay there another day."

He chuckled. "Whoever would think of connecting you with a crime?"

"Oddly enough, I was questioned. There were two

detectives at the hotel. They talked to absolutely everybody."

"And did you confess?"

"No more than you did. Now tell me what happened up north. You were going to Dublin or Belfast. I still don't understand how you detectives go about it. From what I could see, you had nothing to go on. A girl struck down with a golf club."

"Well, there was the other murder, too, remember. Zale."

Wind was riffling the lake surface. Water lapped at the wooden pier. A small sailboat was moored at the end of the dock. A slatted bench had a long rope with life preserver tied to it.

"Let's sit here, Bill. It's a lovely view."

"It sure is. Damn peaceful. Like I thought Rosslare would be."

"Well, are you going to tell me or not? What's the murder of Mr. Zale to do with your trip?"

"Everything. You see, they were tied in together. You look surprised. Well, I was, too. I thought they were separate murders, at first."

"What made you think otherwise?"

"Well, when I was in Dublin, I saw a man who runs a new kind of guerrilla army. Fighting, shooting, robbing, the lot. Terry Dugan. He knew Noreen, you see."

"That girl who was killed – your sister-in-law?"

"Knew her well, too. Said they intended to be married soon."

"Oh, what a pity!"

"Dugan put me on to another man in Noreen's life. Chap who knew her before him. Comes from Galway. George Hanna."

"Hanna? Tall man? I believe I've seen him at the hotel there. Heard him paged. George Hanna, yes."

"So it seemed like one of those old triangles. Two men in love with the same woman. I already knew about another good friend of hers. Muldowney. Runs an antique shop. He and Noreen grew up together. I'd already met Matt Bogson, Noreen's new stepfather, but Terry Dugan told me the old boy had a crush on Noreen himself. You wanted to know how it works. That's how. One complicating factor after another."

"From my meagre knowledge, I'd assumed what a detective needs is evidence."

"That or lack of it."

"Are you serious?"

"It's all a process of elimination. George Hanna might have killed Noreen. Bogson might have. Muldowney or Dugan, too. But for one reason or another, they didn't because somebody else beat them to it."

"Bill Stanwood, now don't be getting cute or cryptic on me. I'm dying to know."

"All right. We'll do lack of evidence first. Zale, the man killed at the caravan, managed the site for Bogson, the owner. Zale was an artist. Needed the job and shelter provided to do his real work. He worked like crazy, doing hundreds upon hundreds of sketches, drawings, paintings. Everybody he ever saw there. The guests of the hotel. The headwaiter, the switchboard girls, the bartender. He had one of you, too. Good likeness."

"Me? I've never met the man, and I'm certain I never posed for him."

"Zale didn't need anybody posing. He saw you on the beach. Sketched you in a bathing suit. Pink bikini. Looking very tan. A lot of you, I might add."

"He didn't! Well, I did have one like that. I suppose he was hiding over the bluff in the high grass."

"Possibly. But he could have just seen you in passing. Drawn you later from memory. He had good recall, you see."

"Okay. You were talking about lack of evidence."

"There was another long-term resident of the caravan site. A Mrs. Gantry. Facing the sea at the end of the lot. Number 8. So here's your lack of evidence. Zale must have seen her some time or other, even though she was an infrequent visitor to her own hut. Yet, although he had pictures of everybody in town or nearby, there were no pictures of Mrs. Gantry."

"Well, how would you know? You've never seen her. Did Zale leave a bitter note to that effect? The only one I missed doing!"

"Most sketches had names on them. Others I recognized. Yours, Doyle's, Bogson. Mrs. Kelly. No, the only one missing apparently was the mysterious Mrs. Gantry who owned a townhouse in Dublin and just visited her wee shack on the sea on impulse."

"Guesswork. I suppose you detectives do a lot of that."

"Sometimes. But then there are the complicating factors I mentioned. I was on the golf course when somebody in a small yellow car fired a shot at one of the golfers. That led me to Wexford and a visit to a Honda dealer, and a car wash. A chap named Muldowney in Enniscorthy nearby owned a similar looking car but he had a bad cold. There was no Kleenex in his car and his Honda was cool, not driven recently."

"My God," she said. "It's a wonder you people solve anything."

"This was easier, because both the Honda dealer and the carwash man could identify the driver of the bogus Honda, meant to be described as Muldowney's. A big, flashy redheaded woman, they agreed. Built like a truck. But with nice legs, one of them said. And a good smile. Knuckle on her nose.

"I went to Zale's hut to trace Noreen's movements. Found him dead and, going through his studio, found a red wig. I took his key and went to number 8 and found a blonde wig. And then I came here."

She looked at him intently. "Are you omitting something?"

"I suppose. Why did you kill Noreen Kelly?"

She said, "What? You must be joking." As they do in cinema.

"The clerk at Hairgoods International in Dublin had your name and address. Made-to-order wigs. For you, not Maureen Gantry. The red wig you dumped at Zale's was left there when you killed him, in case the police tracked down the woman in the yellow car. You neglected to tear out the label. But you did remove all evidence of what Mrs. Gantry looked like. I think you killed Zale to remove the chance of his ever drawing a likeness of the mystery woman in number 8. Later, burned his pictures on the range in your caravan."

"Big, flashy, red-headed broad, you said. Is that me?"

"Not impossible. You were an actress. You're tall. Not difficult to pad yourself up to look topheavy. Knuckle on your nose? A little make-up. You know how. Too bad you've nice legs and didn't wear slacks to hide them."

"Bill, you're mad! Absolutely out-of-your-head mad!"

"Your voice can do tricks, too. You're the one with the masculine voice called Cullimore. Left the message for Noreen to meet George Hanna at the usual place late Friday night. You knew the place because you've spied on them. Evidence of that was the photo of them together that I found in your drawer."

"I can't believe I'm hearing all this from you. You seemed so sane, so, well, unimaginative."

"Listen, lady, you've no idea how a little neat murder stirs up my imagination. Especially of somebody dear to me."

"Well, to be fair about it, your reasons for Mrs. Gantry killing your Mr. Zale sound plausible. If he could identify her, or if she had done something wrong. But why would I want to kill Noreen, that nice sweet girl?"

"You'll have to tell me that. My guess is you were jealous of her, hated her because Hanna had dumped you and still loved Noreen. That's where you and Mrs. Gantry become one, you see. I've been through that little love-palace. Found pictures of all the gents you had there or elsewhere."

"Mrs. Gantry, you mean."

Stanwood sighed. "You were the only one there I didn't ask questions about. Maybe because I was afraid I'd hear something I didn't want to know. You seemed just perfect for me, too good, but desirable now. The headwaiter told me people there came down the same week year after year. You had different times, the only one. I checked at the desk. And you picked this one knowing the VIP tournament was on, a good chance for you to wrap up Hanna, kill him, since you couldn't have him."

"I thought it was Noreen I was supposed to be after."

"I think that was accidental. You knew Hanna was there, it being his week. You went down to arrange his killing, by chance saw Noreen there. She saw you reflected in the glass, and ran off. Later you called Cullimore to bring her out. Called Hanna using her voice to trick him there at the same time. Or used your own, as a threat. You would have killed them both but needed him as a possible suspect, and killed her instead. You'd found his lost club and had it handy. How's that for guesswork?"

"I wonder how it feels to die, not knowing," she said. He saw the little gun slide out of her deep-pocketed skirt. Little .22, he told himself. Hard to kill a man with that. Harder to kill a big man. He was still going on like that in his mind when the little automatic went off with a short snapping sound, like an aborted bark, burning a hole deep in his chest.

Stanwood was surprised to find himself falling backward, taking the wooden bench with him as he tumbled off the dock into the water, seeing her jump aside as he went under.

She stood there a while, waiting for his head to appear, and when it didn't, she sighed, and threw the gun in the water. She was walking back up the hill when she saw the school matron running down toward her.

"There's a call for you, mum. From Dublin. Urgent, they said."

"Thank you, Nora. I'll take it in the office."

"Hello, is this Miss Garner? Miss Mary Garner?"

"Yes, who's calling, please?"

"This is the office of Chief Superintendent Gallagher of the Irish Detective Branch."

"Yes?"

"Is Mr. Stanwood there? Mr. William Stanwood. Like to have a word with him, if it's at all possible."

"I'm sorry, superintendent. He's not here. That is, he's gone."

"Oh, dear. You mean you've killed him, too?"

Forty-Eight

The water was colder than Stanwood expected. The icy shock of it took his mind temporarily off the burning hole in his chest. He put his hand on it. Low enough to have barely missed the right ventricle, he thought. A man needn't die from that. The punctured lung would be something else to reckon with.

The wooden bench he had taken with him as he fell was an accident of fortune. Attached to it on a long rope, the heavy white lifebelt. Really, he couldn't have planned it better, given the circumstances.

He swam deeply, pulling the bench along close to the dock. His shoulder struck one of the thick wooden pilings sunk into the lake bottom, and he clutched at it with his free arm. Slowly he eased his body up the dock support, his other arm looped around the roped lifebelt, hand on his throbbing wound to staunch the flow of blood. Enough had escaped to make the water murky red as he looked up.

He lifted his face, gasping for a quick breath and submerged again. The glance was enough to see her standing directly over him on the narrow slatted dockboards, peering over the side. He waited, came up again for another breath. Lots of bloody red water around me, he thought, watching it flow under the dock. If she doesn't hang around too long, we've got a chance.

She paced the dock for a few steps across and back. Then she stopped and threw something. He saw the gun strike the water. His head was up and clear when she turned and walked back across the boards, her footsteps vibrating overhead, softly diminishing.

Well, Bill, he asked himself, are you man enough to finish the job?

She ran gracefully out of the school door without showing a trace of panic. Her keys were ready when she reached the silvery Mercedes in the circular driveway. The powerful engine coughed and purred as she pulled away. It was on the long and winding gravel path just beyond the gate, when Stanwood lurched up from behind her seat and pressed his .38 Colt Detective Special against her cheek.

He coughed, framing his words in bloody froth. "Drive to the police station, love. I passed it coming through, about five minutes from here, just up the road."

The tea-coloured eyes fastened on his in the rearview glass. "Bill," she said. "I honestly thought you were dead."

The cold heavy metal tapped her cheek gently. "You've got just the five minutes to make it, Mary, or we're both dead."

The easy warming smile, so much a part of her, found its way to her lips again. "You're sure you'd rather not be taken to hospital? It's ever so much closer, Bill."

He cocked the Colt and saw the smile fade. "I'm a cop, baby. Take me where I belong."

Chief Superintendent Gallagher was beaming. "Good work, lad. Your pulling through, I mean. As to how a big man like yourself let a small bullet do such a nasty job, it surprises me no end."

Stanwood, swathed in white binding, grimaced in an abortive chuckle. "Well, sir, as they say, there's nothing faster than a speeding bullet."

Gallagher was unbuttoning his shirt. He stepped closer to the hospital bed, pulled the edges apart, and tapped a faded white scar. "Remarkable, isn't it? Here's proof I was a bit careless myself early on in the going."

"I'll be damned," Stanwood said, whistling softly. "The same spot." His eyes shifted to the burly superintendent's. "Now I've got to ask you, did you get your man?"

Gallagher laughed, shaking his head ruefully. "No, lad, but I got the woman that nearly did me in. Same as you."

"The funny thing is, I could see her side of it, feel sorry for her," Stanwood said gloomily. "Beautiful woman, taller than most men, with more than the usual trouble in finding a man. Rosslare was her great escape, her fantasy life. That's the reason for the wigs. Found somebody each time to romance with, men on the loose away from home. But in the long run, deserting her after the fun and games. Going back home to the wife and kids, the proper life.

"Hanna was her last hope, one she had pinned the most hopes on. And when she discovered he had fallen in love with Noreen, a small girl, the typical woman, she freaked out. So she killed Noreen, hoping to frame Hanna for it, or at least mess up his life. Killing Zale was just another attempt to blur her tracks, remove the last link between her and the lady of the caravan. What she didn't know was that Hanna was nothing to Noreen. She had plenty of other men in her short life."

The super shrugged, throwing out his hands. "Well, they never do figure it all out so that it makes sense, do they?"

Stanwood forced a smile. "Talk about making sense, I was giving myself pep talks on how to get her to marry me."

"Well, lad, to tell the truth," Gallagher said, buttoning his shirt, "I would have done the same with my tiger, given half the chance. Was on the same sticky wicket as yourself."

"What stopped you?"

"No small thing. I was already married, you see."

Yes, Stanwood thought, that would have saved him, too. But now with the sudden blooming promise erased from his life, he was back to where he was before Rosslare. How do you start all over again? he wondered.

"You're welcome to stay with us when you're on your feet," Gallagher was saying. "The wife is a good cook, and Dublin is as good a place as any to be picking up the pieces."

Stanwood nodded slowly. "Well, you know, I just may take you up on that. By God, I think I'm ready."

If you have enjoyed this book and would like to receive details of other Walker mystery titles, please write to:

Mystery Editor
Walker and Company
720 Fifth Avenue
New York, NY 10019